Carey's eyes blazed suddenly

"Your daughter, Mr. Savage," she burst out, "is a flesh-and-blood baby. Small as she is, she needs your love. Please let me bring her to you—one look at her would change your attitude completely."

"My attitude," Patrick interrupted harshly, "is entirely my own business, as is the way I conduct my relationship with my daughter, or any other female, Miss Armitage."

Carey's chin went up in defiance. "My sole interest, I can assure you, is in the relationship you don't have with your baby daughter. I do my best, and while I love her very much . . ." She stopped suddenly, conscious of what she was saying.

"Well, well," drawled Patrick Savage. "What a passionate creature you are, after all, Nanny, dear—not nearly as self-contained as you'd have us believe."

Catherine George was born in Wales, and
following her marriage to an engineer, lived in
Brazil for eight years at a gold-mine site. It was an
experience she would later draw upon for her
books, when she and her husband returned to
England. Now her husband helps manage their
household so that Catherine can devote more time
to her writing. They have two children, a daughter
and a son, who share their mother's love of
language and writing.

Books by Catherine George

HARLEQUIN ROMANCE

2535—RELUCTANT PARAGON
2571—DREAM OF MIDSUMMER
2720—DESIRABLE PROPERTY
2822—THE FOLLY OF LOVING
2924—MAN OF IRON
2942—THIS TIME ROUND
3081—CONSOLATION PRIZE
3129—ARROGANT INTERLOPER

HARLEQUIN PRESENTS

1016—LOVE LIES SLEEPING
1065—TOUCH ME IN THE MORNING
1152—VILLAIN OF THE PIECE
1184—TRUE PARADISE
1225—LOVEKNOT
1255—EVER SINCE EDEN
1321—COME BACK TO ME

A CIVILISED ARRANGEMENT

Catherine George

Harlequin Books

TORONTO • NEW YORK • LONDON
AMSTERDAM • PARIS • SYDNEY • HAMBURG
STOCKHOLM • ATHENS • TOKYO • MILAN

Original hardcover edition published in 1990
by Mills & Boon Limited

ISBN 0-373-03147-5

Harlequin Romance first edition September 1991

A CIVILISED ARRANGEMENT

CHAPTER ONE

CAREY woke, as she always did, at the first faint wail of protest. In a flash she was out of bed and on her way into the adjoining room, her smile indulgent as she lifted the baby out of the cot to cuddle the small, warm body close for a moment or two, murmuring, soothing, before beginning the familiar ritual of making her dry and comfortable. The diminutive Alice made soft bubbling noises, thrusting minuscule fingers in her mouth as Carey changed her and cocooned her securely in her blanket then sat down with her little bundle on a low chair near the cot.

'Now,' she said softly, 'this is just a drink of water, honeybun. No more two o'clock feeds, remember. Supper at ten, then nothing until breakfast. OK?' She smiled as the baby began sucking voraciously on the teat of the bottle. The little face crumpled for an instant as Alice tasted water instead of milk; Carey held her breath, but the sucking resumed, and eventually the eyelids drooped silky fans of lashes on petal-soft cheeks, the little body relaxed, boneless, and at last the rosebud mouth relinquished the teat and Alice was asleep again.

With practised deftness Carey lowered the baby into the cot and covered her up, then stood for a while, watching over her until she was sure Alice was asleep before she crept from the room, feeling ominously wide awake now, as she so often did at this hour. She put on her dressing-gown, took another look at the sleeping baby, then went silently from the room, knowing of old that a hot drink was the only hope of getting some rest before Alice's interior alarm clock went off again at six.

The silent house felt very empty as Carey stole down the stairs. There was scarcely need for a light. Moonlight poured through the stained-glass window in the hall, creating jewelled lozenges of light on the mosaic floor. Unfortunately it also transformed the suit of armour in the corner into a disturbing figure of menace, and Carey scurried down the last three steps to turn on another light, in sudden need of man-made illumination, solely, as she knew perfectly well, because it was Dilys's night off and her own first time alone at night in Llynglas. As she fled in silent retreat down the long passage towards the kitchen, she badly missed having the housekeeper on the premises. Which was totally illogical, she told herself firmly, since Dilys slept in a self-contained apartment over the kitchen, in a different wing of the house altogether. Nevertheless tonight, with only the baby for company, Carey felt a lot more vulnerable than usual.

Laughing at herself, she flung open the kitchen door then stopped dead in her tracks. All her amorphous fears knotted together in a ball of terror which stuck in her throat, rendering her dumb at the sight of the room ablaze with lights and a man sitting on the large table in the middle of the room, a mug of steaming coffee in one hand and an enormously thick sandwich in the other. He stared at her in blank astonishment, equally dumbstruck. Time seemed suspended. Then Carey's common sense resumed its normal service, pointing out that no self-respecting burglar would take time off for a coffee-break in the middle of breaking and entering. After which it also pointed out that the man was very good-looking in a haggard sort of way, and that bare feet, a thin cotton dressing-gown and hair hanging down her back were not exactly the best of wear for repelling intruders.

'Who the hell,' said the man, in a drawling, husky voice, 'are you?'

Carey squared her shoulders, standing her ground. 'Shouldn't I be asking *you* that?'

He eyed her up and down in a leisurely sort of way, then put down his coffee and sandwich and slid off the table to walk towards her. Carey dodged back instinctively, but he shook his head in mock reproof.

'I don't bite, girl. And I don't really need permission to make myself a snack in my own kitchen, either. You must be new here. Do you come in from the village to help Dilys?'

Carey's heart plummeted to somewhere near her knees. 'I'm so sorry,' she managed, her voice hoarse with dismay. 'You must be Mr Savage.'

He nodded thoughtfully. 'The very same. Patrick Savage, newly arrived from California, stupid with jet lag and rather hungry. Otherwise quite harmless, I assure you.'

'How do you do?' replied Carey with what dignity she could muster. 'I'm the nanny your mother engaged to look after your daughter, Mr Savage.'

The change in Patrick Savage was startling. His face, tanned to the colour of old leather by the Californian sun, set in harsh, ageing lines, and his eyes, deep-set and of a surprising soot-black against his sun-bleached hair, filled with pain for an instant then drained of expression as he turned to pick up his mug of coffee.

'Ah, yes,' he said, his back to Carey. 'My daughter. I came straight here—I haven't contacted my mother yet. I thought the child was still in hospital.'

Carey eyed the broad back without favour. She had learned the bare facts of the tragedy of Alice's birth from the baby's grandmother, but up to now had firmly believed Mrs Savage to be exaggerating her son's lack of interest in his child. Evidently not.

'Although born prematurely Alice has made rapid progress, Mr Savage,' Carey informed him crisply. 'She was able to leave hospital much sooner than anticipated.'

He turned to face her. 'Odd that my mother saw fit to keep me in the dark about it.'

'I gather,' said Carey, choosing her words with care, 'that she thought it best for me to travel here to Llynglas and settle Alice in before you came home.'

'Best for whom, I wonder?' he said bitterly. 'My mother, young woman, is an incurable romantic— quite convinced that one look at the child will transform me into a besotted, doting father.' He gave a short, unamused laugh. 'Sorry. Not fair to embroil you in family arguments.' He gazed at her in silence for some moments. 'What on earth possessed a girl like you to bury yourself in a place like Llynglas? You can't have been short of more tempting prospects. I thought trained nannies were scarce as hens' teeth.'

'I don't consider it "burying", Mr Savage,' she said coolly. 'I've worked in London for several years. I welcomed a post in the country for a change.' To her embarrassment a yawn got the better of her, and Patrick Savage frowned.

'Go back to bed,' he said shortly. 'You must be a hell of a sight more exhausted than I am. What sort of time does the child get you up in the morning?'

'*Alice,*' said Carey pointedly, 'generally wakes at six.'

Patrick Savage shuddered. 'Barbaric—and why Alice, for heaven's sake?'

Carey didn't even try to hide her disapproval. 'Your mother chose it, Mr Savage. Elinor Alice, after herself.'

Elinor Alice's father was so patently uninterested in this piece of information that Carey bade him a very formal goodnight, overcome with sudden longing for her bed.

'Just a minute,' he said as she opened the door. 'While we're on the subject of names, how am I supposed to address you? Nanny?'

'If you wish.'

'How about your last employers?'

Carey turned to look at him. 'I was with an American family. They preferred first names.'

He returned the look for rather longer than Carey would have liked, rubbing a hand over his dark-stubbled jaw. 'I see. Goodnight, then. Leave the child with Dilys some time tomorrow afternoon, would you? I've got a few ground-rules I'd like to lay down, so come up to my study about four.'

Patrick Savage dismissed her with a cool nod and turned away, leaving Carey to take herself out of the kitchen and trudge upstairs to salvage what remained of the night.

Sending up a silent prayer of thanks when she found Alice still sleeping peacefully, Carey slid into bed, then lay staring at the moonlight through the window, feeling restless and thoroughly irritable after the surprise encounter with her new employer. The hot drink had never materialised, either, she thought crossly. All in all, her first meeting with Patrick Savage had been a total disaster. She knew something about him, of course, mainly because he was a writer whose novels and plays were consistently successful. And at the interview Mrs Savage had made it clear that her son's motive for burying himself in the wilds of Wales was a commission to write the teleplay for his latest block-busting novel.

Carey turned over restlessly, punching her pillow. Odd, really, she thought. He wasn't a bit what she'd expected—years younger, for a start. No photograph ever appeared on the dust-jackets of his novels which, of course, Carey thought wryly, was why she'd conjured up a man somewhere between Heathcliff and Mr Rochester, all tormented features and wild black hair and eyes. Patrick Savage's

eyes filled the bill admirably, but otherwise her first
startled impression in the kitchen had been of a
California beach-boy, all sun-bleached hair and
deep-dyed tan and those long, long legs which had
swung to and fro as he'd sat on the kitchen table
staring at her. Admittedly the torment in his eyes
had been plain enough when she'd mentioned Alice.
Only of course it hadn't been for the baby, Carey
thought with compassion. Poor little Alice was only
a reminder that her birth had cost Patrick Savage
his wife, Stephanie.

Elinor Alice Savage proved just how model a baby
she could be by sleeping until almost seven next
morning, for which Carey was deeply grateful.
Numb with sleep, she was all fingers and thumbs
for once, and took much longer than usual to bathe
and dress the baby, after which it was a blessed relief
to sit down to give Alice her first bottle of the day.
By the time Carey had taken the baby downstairs
and installed her in the large, old-fashioned perambulator in the courtyard, Miss Dilys Howells was
just descending from a muddy pick-up at the other
end of the causeway on the shore of Llynglas, which
this perfect June morning was doing its best to live
up to its translation of 'blue lake'.

The buxom, dark-haired little woman came hurrying along the causeway and under the portcullis
of the gate-tower, her round face beaming as she
greeted Carey then bent to inspect the small face
beneath the white net protecting Alice from the local
insect population.

'There's my beautiful,' said Dilys dotingly, then turned to Carey. 'Which is more than I can say for you, my girl. Terrible shadows under your eyes! Bad night with the baby?'

Carey explained as they went inside. Dilys was incensed when she heard that 'Mr Patrick' had arrived unexpectedly during the night.

'Must have frightened you to death, *cariad*—whatever was he thinking of, not letting me know he was coming?'

'He didn't even tell Mrs Savage,' said Carey, as she sliced bread for toast. 'Nor did he know anything about me.' She described her own shock at finding Patrick Savage enjoying a snack on the table she was now laying for breakfast.

Dilys was deeply put out by her employer's unexpected arrival at Llynglas. 'No help for it—I'll have to take something out of the freezer for his dinner,' she said with annoyance. 'I was going to make shepherd's pie for you and me, Carey, from the remains of that leg of lamb, but I can't give Mr Patrick that.'

Carey grinned teasingly as she spread marmalade on her toast. 'I don't see why not.'

Dilys's rosy face flushed a deeper hue. 'He can have some for his lunch, certainly, but I can't give Mr Patrick shepherd's pie for his dinner, girl!'

Carey laughed, assuring the bustling little woman that whatever she cooked was delicious, but that any preparations for dinner would have to be disrupted during the afternoon, anyway, to include a session of baby-sitting at four, when Mr Savage required an interview with the nanny. 'Wants to check my credentials, I expect—I don't suppose I impressed him in my dressing-gown with my hair all over the place.'

After breakfast Carey wheeled Alice into the rose garden below her bedroom window, with the aim of keeping an eye on her while she tidied the rooms allotted to her use. By the time her few chores were done Carey noticed that Alice was showing signs of waking up, and she ran downstairs to give her a drink in the kitchen with Dilys, then set off with the baby for her usual walk.

Carey pushed the big perambulator under the portcullis of the gate-tower then along the causeway which led from the Savage household across the blue waters of the lake to the shore. Pine-trees and deciduous woodland edged the perimeter of the lake, but where the causeway met the shore the woodland parted to give way to gardens laid out in park-like splendour, with smooth green lawns and brilliant, flower-filled beds with never a weed in sight. Carey pushed the pram past lilied pools and cascading waterfalls, then along the famous walk where classical statues languished between tall sentinel yews en route to a fountain where apocryphal fish spouted jets of glittering water high into the air.

Carey never ceased to marvel at the extravagant bravura of the man who had dreamed up the gardens of Llynglas, which for the moment she had to herself, except for the men working in them. She waved as she passed, receiving shy smiles in return, the friendliest from Gwilym Davies, the head gardener who lived in the lodge and acted as watchman and caretaker and even money collector when the gardens opened to the public in spring and summer.

'Mr Patrick's back, then, Miss Carey,' he observed, as he bent to smile at the baby. 'What did he think of this young lady?'

'He hasn't seen her yet. He's still sleeping off his jet lag.'

Carey exchanged a few pleasantries, then continued with her walk, wondering just how much was known locally about the background to Alice's birth. All she knew herself was that Patrick Savage's wife, Stephanie, better known on stage and television screen by her professional name of Drake, had not survived Alice's premature birth, and Patrick, bereft and grief-stricken, had fled to America to a California beach house loaned by a friend in the film industry. And there he had stayed, leaving all arrangements for his daughter to his mother, remaining incommunicado right up to his startling appearance in the kitchen of Llynglas the night before.

Mrs Savage had been very frank with Carey at the interview in her handsome Knightsbridge flat. At seventy-five, troubled with arthritis, she was, she had said firmly, not the right person to take charge of the baby herself. And even if she had been, she had added, sighing, she still felt it was by far the best thing for Patrick to have care of the child himself, with the right help.

Carey, Norland College training and several years' experience apart, had proved to be just what Mrs Savage had been looking for, not merely because the other woman had taken to her on sight, but because of her willingness to live in a remote part of Wales far from the most modest of city lights.

'The other applicants,' Mrs Savage had informed Carey wryly, 'more or less turned tail and ran when I came to that bit. I hope very much that *you* won't, Miss Armitage, because I fancy you're just the person I'm looking for to take care of my granddaughter.'

One way and another the job had been very much to Carey's taste: an excellent salary, only one small baby to take care of, no mother to interfere and—most important of all—a complete change of scene.

And no scene could be more different than this one, thought Carey in amusement as she turned the pram in the direction of the actual dwelling of Llynglas. Mrs Savage had refrained from any precise description of her son's country retreat, her dry sense of humour leaving Llynglas to make its own impact on Carey on her arrival. Its extraordinary beauty was still breathtaking after seeing it every day for the past fortnight, but that first evening, as the hired car had conveyed Carey and her tiny charge through the gardens of Llynglas and along the carriageway to the water's edge, she had gazed in utter wonder at the miniature ruined castle floating in the middle of the lake. Carey had looked about her in vain for the country house she'd been expecting, her eyes almost starting from her head as the chauffeur had driven straight on to the causeway linking the castle to the shore, taking his passengers under the portcullis of the gate-tower dominating the ruined walls, before drawing up in the courtyard of a miniature castle complete with crenellated roof and adjoining tower.

'Somewhere between Walt Disney and Ruritania,' Carey had written later to her brother and his wife. 'I thought I was dreaming when I actually laid eyes on Llynglas—as though I'd actually brought Alice to live in Wonderland! It's actually a custom-built ruin—a folly built by a Victorian forebear of my present employer. Mr Theophilus Savage made his fortune in iron and built Llynglas as a monument to his success. It's quite unbelievable. I wouldn't be at all surprised if a hand came up out of the lake any moment, brandishing Excalibur, or even if Owain Glyndwr materialised out of the mist to defend his beloved Wales from the English intruders. If he does, of course, I'll tell him my mother was a Carey from Pembrokeshire, and I'll be as safe as home-grown Dilys, housekeeper *par excellence* and spinster of this parish.'

Which last bit, thought Carey bleakly as she pushed the pram across the causeway, could just as well apply to me. Not this particular parish, of course, but a single lady she was likely to remain, just the same, for the term of her natural life.

'Mr Savage still asleep?' inquired Carey casually as she ate her lunch in the kitchen with Dilys.

'I took him up a tray, but he wouldn't touch a thing. Proper grumpy, he was,' said Dilys disapprovingly. 'Told me to wake him at three-thirty and send you up at four.'

'So he hasn't forgotten I'm here, then.'

'No, indeed. Mr Patrick never forgets a thing. More's the pity,' added Dilys, sighing. 'There's some things *better* forgotten, believe me.'

Carey changed the subject hastily. The last thing she wanted was any involvement with the Savage family's private concerns. She was here solely to look after Alice. Nothing else. She felt sorry for Patrick Savage, of course. Anyone with a shred of humanity would feel the same. An image leapt in her mind, unbidden, of her first sight of Patrick Savage, seated here on this very kitchen table with the overhead light gleaming on his bright blond hair. He was, she admitted reluctantly, a very attractive man, but as far as she was concerned this was merely a point in his disfavour. To her the term 'attractive man' was synonymous with grief and heartbreak; something—or someone—to avoid like the plague. She came to with a start as she realised Dilys was offering her some damson tart for pudding.

'Sorry, I was miles away—and delicious though that looks I don't think so, thanks just the same.'

'Too tired to eat, by the look of you,' said Dilys with concern. 'Take the baby up for her nap and have a lie down yourself while she's asleep. I'll see you're up in plenty of time to talk to Mr Patrick.'

Carey thanked her as she lifted Alice out of the pram. 'I think I will for once, Dilys. Would you give me a knock just to make sure I'm up, though, please?' She pulled a face. 'I'd like to look a bit tidier when I confront Mr Savage this time.'

Carey took more pains with her appearance than usual, satisfied she looked pin-neat and efficient by

the time she was ready to face Patrick Savage in his
lair in the tower. She hadn't been able to settle to
a nap after all. She'd relaxed in the bath instead,
letting the water go cold while she'd gone on with
her second reading of the novel Patrick Savage was
here in Llynglas to adapt for television. Even second
time round Carey had found herself deeply en-
grossed in the story of four college students and
their various careers in the outwide world, the
women they loved and/or married, and the major
political scandal which cast a long shadow over all
their lives. The writing was brilliant, but cynicism
and disillusionment ran through the book like a
dark ribbon intertwined with the woven fabric of
the plot, leaving Carey in a decidedly melancholy
frame of mind as she'd dressed in readiness for the
coming interview.

Carey had never been asked to wear a uniform
in her former posts, but she was in the habit of
keeping three or four neat, serviceable dresses for
summer wear, crisp shirtwaisters in washable
cottons or linens, worn with good leather shoes,
mostly flat-heeled for walking with prams and
running about after toddlers. She decided the interview with Patrick Savage called for one of the
new dresses, in cotton the colour of the terracotta
pots outside in the courtyard. The shade flattered
her olive skin and added to the gloss of colour along
her high cheek-bones, her healthy look one of the
bonuses of hours spent pram-pushing in the fresh
air of Llynglas. Her long hair, which was the dense,
Celtic black of her Carey forebears, she brushed
back as usual into the neat, heavy coil she kept to

during working hours, without a single tendril to soften the features she knew were regular and well-defined enough to take it, just as the bright slate-grey of her almond-shaped eyes needed nothing to emphasise them at this time of day. She allowed herself a touch of lipstick, then picked up the baby and cuddled her for a minute or two, before taking her down to Dilys.

'You look a lot better,' remarked that lady with satisfaction.

'Had a bath,' said Carey briefly, tucking in a soft woolly lamb alongside Alice in the pram.

Dilys chortled. 'I'd have my second one today this minute if I thought it would make me look like that, *cariad*!' She glanced at the clock. 'Off you go, then. It's almost four.'

When Carey's climb up the spiral staircase brought her to the second floor of the tower, she found a door salvaged from a far older building than Theophilus Savage's whimsical folly. Entry to Patrick Savage's study was barred by heavy timbers, ancient and weathered from centuries of use, with massive hinges of wrought iron, like the great ring which served as a handle. The entire door would have looked more in place outside a monk's cell, thought Carey as she looked it over. Which was an incongruous idea. She'd been in Patrick Savage's company only a brief time the night before, it was true. But if Patrick Savage was of a monastic turn of mind she'd eat her Norland diploma.

'Come in,' barked a peremptory voice as Carey tapped on the door, and she turned the handle, pushed open the door and found herself in a circular apartment which formed the middle section of the tower. Four pointed Gothic windows let in light all round a room lined from floor to ceiling with books. A thin Afghan rug glowed on the polished boards of the floor, a word processor sat, as expected, on a sturdy, leather-topped table between two of the windows, and behind a large partners' desk, with drawers back and front, sat Patrick Savage, looking very different from the man of the early hours of the morning.

He rose as Carey entered, and held out his hand across the desk. 'Good afternoon. I trust you managed to get *some* rest last night?'

'Yes, thank you, Mr Savage.' Carey clasped his hand briefly, then took the chair he indicated, which had been placed so that light from one of the windows fell full on her face. She looked across the desk at her new employer, waiting for him to begin on a catechism about her credentials, noting that there was no trace of California beach-boy about him today. His hair was damp from a recent shower, its sleekness the colour of expensive butterscotch above a face only marginally less haggard than the previous night. Despite his spectacular tan, smudges of fatigue showed like bruises beneath the eyes he trained on her face with impersonal curiosity. Carey bore his scrutiny with composure, her hands clasped loosely in her lap as she waited for him to begin.

As expected, Patrick Savage's opening questions were about her impeccable qualifications, which were from the National Nursery Examination Board and the Royal Society of Health; also the Norland

Diploma itself, attained only after nine months' satisfactory work in her first post.

'Very impressive,' he commented, eyeing the CV in front of him. 'My mother posted this on to me here, of course, but when I rang her this morning she told me she was satisfied you were just the person to have care of—of the child, under the circumstances.' He stopped and shot a hard, glittering look across the desk. 'I assume you're in full possession of my particular "circumstances"?'

'No, Mr Savage—only of Alice's.' Carey met his eyes serenely. 'I was, of course, informed that her mother died when she was born. After spending her first three months in hospital Alice has been in my charge now for six weeks, four of which were spent in Mrs Savage's flat in Knightsbridge before I travelled down here with Alice by car.'

'Very succinct.' Patrick Savage returned to the letter in front of him. 'My mother says she's left arrangements about time off to me, that I must agree with whatever you require, also that I must arrange for someone else to look after the child in your absence.'

'That won't be necessary for the time being, Mr Savage.'

He looked up. 'You'll need *some* time away from this place, I imagine, Miss Carey!'

'A few hours in Welshpool on my day off will be all I require for the present,' Carey informed him, 'and for that Dilys can manage very well. Megan—Mrs Pugh, who comes in from the village, will take over Dilys's domestic duties on those occasions. I feel it's very important for Alice to have the security of familiar people around her at this stage. Since she——' Carey hesitated, then went on carefully. 'Since Alice is motherless, I will do my best to function as a maternal substitute, give her as much affection and continuity as possible, with Dilys as a willing assistant when necessary. If that meets with your approval,' she added belatedly, with a placatory smile at the set face across the desk.

Patrick Savage made no response for a moment, his face dark and expressionless under hair displaying tow-coloured streaks as it dried. 'How easy you make it sound,' he said at last.

Carey looked at him questioningly. 'Easy?'

'To provide mother-love with such facility.'

'If I didn't find it easy to love babies, Mr Savage, I'd be in quite the wrong job!'

'What prompted a girl like you to become a nanny?' he asked.

Something in his phrasing irritated Carey. 'I always wanted to work with children,' she said coolly, 'but instead of teaching I chose this particular branch of childcare.'

'No desire for higher things—in the way of education and a career, I mean?'

'It all depends, I suppose, on what interpretation one places on "higher things", Mr Savage,' she returned, refusing to let him ruffle her. 'From my point of view I'm doing the thing I'm most suited to do, providing a very necessary service for which I receive adequate payment in return.'

'Adequate!' he snorted. 'You're bloody expensive, Miss Carey.'

'No more than normal under the circumstances,' she said, finding it harder by the minute to be civil.

'You get free bed, board and a very respectable salary as pure pocket-money, as far as I can see!'

'True. But in return I work hours no other employee would even consider,' she reminded him politely. 'And often with very little sleep, especially when my charge is as young as your daughter.'

'Oh, I'm not quibbling,' he said, losing interest. 'I'm sure you'll earn every penny of it.' He frowned suddenly as he noted something on her CV. 'You're a lot older than I thought you were. Twenty-four, it says here.'

She inclined her head.

'Last night,' he went on, his eyes lighting with sudden, startling warmth, 'I thought you were about fifteen. Must have been the bare feet and the hair.' He gestured towards her faultless black coil. 'Puts years on you like that, you know.'

'But practical in my line of work, Mr Savage,' she said pleasantly, and made to rise. 'Is that all?'

'No. Sit down again, please.' Patrick Savage leaned back in his chair. 'I'd like to know a little about your background, if you don't mind. What about your family? Won't they object if you don't take time off to visit them?'

'My parents are dead, Mr Savage. Otherwise I've only the one brother, a doctor, in Cardiff. I've just spent a fairly lengthy period at his home recently, looking after my little nephew while my sister-in-law recovered from a back injury.' She smiled a little. 'I'm sure they'll exist without seeing me for a while.'

He nodded. 'I see. Feel free to ring them whenever you want, of course.'

'Thank you, but I make it a rule to keep the telephone for emergencies. I prefer to write letters.'

'Exemplary!' He eyed her in silence for a moment. 'By the way, just to complete the picture I think you'd better tell me whether some ardent lover's likely to carry you off to a life of bliss at a moment's notice. I'd need due warning, if only to make other arrangements.'

Carey would have given much to tell him to mind his own business, but conquered the urge, even managing a civil tone as she told him she would, of course, give adequate notice should such an unlikely event occur. 'Nevertheless,' she added, 'the question doesn't arise. There is no one. Nor is there likely to be.'

Patent disbelief lit the intelligent black eyes. 'No men?'

Carey shook her head. 'None, Mr Savage.'

He frowned. 'Pretty unlikely, isn't it? You're a good-looking lady, Miss Carey. And you like babies. Don't you fancy marrying some guy and having a few of your own?'

His words cut her to the heart. 'Marriage isn't every woman's goal, Mr Savage,' she said stonily.

'Besides which you consider it's none of my damned business,' he said with surprising good humour, and turned to the papers clipped to Carey's CV. 'Your references are positively glowing. From the raptures of your last employers—the American diplomatic family, I assume—I'm surprised they could bear to part with you!'

'My sister-in-law needed me. The Stephensons were returning to Washington at the time, in any case.'

'Didn't they want you to go with them?'

'Yes, they did.'

Patrick Savage eyed her curiously. 'I would have thought a girl like you would have jumped at the chance.'

'I prefer to work in this country, Mr Savage.'

'Which, of course, is my good fortune,' he said, his attractive drawl very pronounced as he raised an eyebrow at her. 'There can't be many young women with your credentials prepared to immure themselves in a place like this.'

'Immure being the word,' said Carey before she could stop herself, and he smiled.

'Very true. Walls, ruined or otherwise, enclose us at Llynglas!' He sobered, his manner abruptly businesslike. 'Now. Let's get down to brass tacks. There are one or two things I must make crystal-clear to you, Miss Carey.'

She waited, irritated slightly by his mistake over her name.

'Because,' he began with care, 'the child was born under such unhappy circumstances, it's important you understand from the start that I feel none of the normal paternal feelings I imagine are customary for a new father.' He looked up from beneath his brows suddenly, locking his eyes with hers. 'I have a job to do here, a deadline to meet. This precludes any attempt at the relationship I'm sure you feel I should try to establish with the scrap of humanity entitled to call herself my daughter.'

Which statement made Carey long to assault her employer across his valuable antique desk. The man didn't deserve such a beautiful baby.

'In short,' he continued, 'I would be obliged, Miss Carey, if you could organise things so that I don't come into contact with the child at all if possible. It's your job to make sure I never hear her crying, or look down on her perambulator in the courtyard. Keep it to the knot garden or the rose garden, please. Neither of those is visible from here.'

'I take her for a walk once, sometimes twice, every day,' Carey reminded him, concealing her resentment. 'It's not physically possible to reach the causeway without passing through the courtyard.'

'I realise that,' he said impatiently. 'I meant I don't want the child left there to sleep in the sun as she was today.'

'Very well,' said Carey. 'Is that all, Mr Savage?'

'Not quite.' Patrick Savage stood up, giving himself the advantage of about a foot of superior height as Carey rose to go. 'You may have the entire run of the main house, of course, but this tower is off-limits. No one comes up here but Dilys. Is that clear?'

'Perfectly.'

'Good. That's it, then, Miss Carey, unless you have any comments to make?'

'No, Mr Savage.' Or none, she thought bitterly, she could make and still keep her job. She walked straight-backed to the door, then turned to look at him. 'One insignificant detail. Carey is my first name. If you prefer to address me as "Miss", it should be Armitage.'

Patrick Savage looked blank for a moment, then turned to the CV on the desk. When he looked up again his eyes held the same unsettling warmth he'd shown for a moment earlier on, and Carey stiffened, suspicious of it after his unbelievable remarks about his baby daughter.

'So it is. I'm sorry. I just caught sight of the "Carey" bit and didn't look further. Unpardonable to get a lady's name wrong,' he drawled, his smile deepening. 'But isn't Carey a surname, anyway?'

'Yes—my mother's.'

'Do I have your permission to use it?'

How satisfying it would have been to refuse! 'If you wish,' she said without inflexion. 'Good afternoon, Mr Savage.'

CHAPTER TWO

CAREY'S first job had been with an energetic young couple who had run their own advertising agency. She had been treated as one of the family, with little employer-employee friction, and had left only when young Lucinda had gone away to school.

From the friendly young Worthings, Carey had gone directly to the Stephensons, who had been in the American diplomatic service. But although Carey had had her own self-contained little apartment in the rented house near the American Embassy, Ellen Stephenson had insisted from the first that Carey must think of herself as part of the family, and join them each evening at dinner when there were no guests. Dean and Abby had been lively toddlers when Carey had first taken them in her charge, but by the time she'd left they had possessed marked British accents and had been ready for their new school in Washington when they returned Stateside.

Ellen had pleaded with Carey to accompany them to the States when they returned, but at that juncture Jenny Armitage had hurt her back, little Paul Armitage had been only a few weeks old, and Carey had felt she had had no choice but to decline the opportunity to see life in the United States of America.

There was a wry twist to Carey's mouth as she reflected that at Llynglas there was no question of living as one of the family. For one thing there *was* no family, as such. Patrick Savage lived cut off from the world in his ivory tower, Dilys Howells ruled the domestic front, and Carey occupied a sort of no-man's land somewhere in between. The rooms she and Alice occupied had been guest rooms in former, more sociable days, and were quite beautiful. But Carey ate her meals with Dilys in the kitchen, and Patrick Savage dined in the tower in solitary state, which meant that Dilys toiled up the stone spiral to the study three times a day with her master's meals on a tray.

'I think it's inconsiderate,' said Carey, a few days after the interview with Patrick Savage. 'He shouldn't expect you to run up and down those stairs.'

'I don't run, love. And I don't mind at all.' Dilys looked up from the pastry she was rolling. 'Otherwise he'd have to make time to come down to eat in the dining-room on the ground floor of the tower.'

'Easier for you,' commented Carey.

'But he doesn't stop for food, you see, Carey. I put the tray on the desk and he goes on clattering on the keys and staring at the screen of that machine of his while he eats. I swear he doesn't taste a mouthful of it.'

'Ungrateful man. He doesn't deserve a cook like you!' Carey hoisted the baby against her shoulder, patting her gently. 'It can't be good for him, though, shut up there all the time in the place where——' She stopped, flushing. 'I wasn't prying, Dilys, honestly. But if his wife died here you'd think it would be the last place he'd want to be.'

Dilys looked taken aback. 'Oh, but she didn't die here, *cariad*! Mr Patrick inherited this place quite recently. His wife only came down here just the once for a weekend. She passed away in London, poor lady—went into premature labour while Mr Patrick was out making one of them after-dinner speeches. He was called away to the hospital, and she died a few hours later, I believe.'

Carey stared at the other woman, harrowed. 'Oh, Dilys, how sad!' She hugged the baby tighter, filled with a sudden fierce desire to compensate the child not only for the mother-love lost to her, but for the other, paternal love Patrick Savage deliberately withheld.

She was thoughtful as she wheeled Alice on her afternoon walk over the causeway, past the black Porsche which hadn't moved from its place in the courtyard since Patrick Savage's arrival. It was the only evidence that he was actually in residence, because she'd seen nothing of him since their interview in the tower. She heard him regularly enough. It was his habit to go for a run every night after dark, along this very causeway, where she could hear his feet crunching on the gravel as his long legs went flying towards the shore and the gardens, where, according to Dilys, he pounded round the ornamental acres some nights, or on others ran along the narrow mountain road that twisted up into the lonely distance northwest of Llynglas.

'Says it keeps him fit,' Dilys had commented with a sniff.

Carey found herself wondering, as she often did, about the grief so bitter that it could motivate a man like Patrick Savage to cut himself off from all human contact. She felt sympathy for his grief, of course, but none at all for his refusal to make contact with a baby so adorable her nanny found her totally irresistible. With a painful tug at her heartstrings Carey smiled lovingly at Alice, who was making little indistinct sounds of communication as she waved her tiny starfish hands above the light rug which covered her. The day was cold for June. Carey had abandoned her cotton dresses for a dark blue tracksuit, having decided that since she never laid eyes on her employer it hardly seemed to matter what clothes she chose to wear, as long as they were sensible and appropriate for the weather.

Carey's brows knitted as she remembered Patrick Savage's questions about her background. It was only to be expected, of course. Any father would want to make sure his daughter's welfare was in the hands of someone suitable. But Patrick Savage wasn't any old father—far from it. Unlike her previous posts, where the fathers had adored their children, P. Savage, Esq. wouldn't even look at his baby.

'And you're so gorgeous, too,' Carey told Alice. 'Your daddy doesn't know what he's missing. You're the best baby in the world, and I love you to bits, even if your famous father doesn't!'

A sudden squall of rain meant that Carey had to snap the hood up on the pram and secure the waterproof apron in place, an arrangement which impeded Alice's view of the world and met with her strong disapproval.

'I know, I know,' said Carey apologetically, as she bowled the pram back to Llynglas to an accompaniment of indignant cries, 'but I can't have you getting wet, honeybun, so you'll just have to put up with it.'

The heavens opened with such force that Carey was soaked through by the time she reached the causeway, where the waters of the lake whipped up on either side in rather unpleasant proximity as she pushed the pram at top speed towards the gate-tower, buffeting poor Alice inside to a degree which made her roar with surprising volume for a small baby. As Carey arrived panting in the courtyard, her eyes flew to an open window in the tower, where a tall figure stood sentinel, gazing down at her, and Carey retreated hurriedly, pushing the pram round to the kitchen door out of sight of that brooding black stare, eager to get her squalling charge out of sight and sound of her father.

'She objected to being jet-propelled on the way home,' said Carey breathlessly, as she surrendered the incensed Alice to Dilys.

'Leave her to me,' commanded Dilys. 'Just you get those wet clothes off at once, my girl!'

When Carey emerged from her bedroom a few minutes later, slightly damp about the hair but otherwise neat in a crisp shirtwaister dress, she was startled to see a tall figure lounging against the stone balustrade outside on the landing. Patrick Savage looked oddly alien against his Gothic background in a thick white sweater and Levis, with American-style saddle shoes on long, bare brown feet, hair gleaming silver-gilt in the gloom.

'Oh—good afternoon, Mr Savage,' she said, taken off guard at the sight of him. 'Is something wrong?'

Patrick Savage shook his head, subjecting her to a long, leisurely scrutiny from head to toe, then his smile gleamed white in his dark face. 'Much more suitable. The creature I just saw doing an Olympic sprint across the causeway wasn't much like my idea of the perfect nanny. I thought they wore starchy dresses and pork-pie hats, not tracksuits.'

'If you'd prefer the former, of course I'll comply,' returned Carey, recovering quickly. 'I forgot to ask your views on uniform the other day.'

'I was kidding,' he said wearily. 'Wear what you like. Lord knows you were dressed exactly right for this bloody awful weather.' He turned moodily to stare through the great window. 'The rain's sheeting down now—good thing you turned back when you did.' He fell in step with her as they went down to the hall, where the sound of Alice's protestations were all too audible, even from behind the closed kitchen door.

'Is she always as noisy as this?' asked Patrick edgily.

'No. On the whole your daughter's a very good baby—far better than the others I've looked after,' Carey assured him. 'I'm sorry if she's disturbing you, but one can't switch a baby off like a machine, Mr Savage.'

'Something you must regret, I should think, if she does that in the middle of the night!'

Carey's eyes blazed suddenly. 'Your daughter, Mr Savage,' she burst out, 'is a flesh-and-blood baby—a tiny human being, with needs as pressing and important as yours or anyone else's. Small as she is, she needs your love even *more* than a baby in normal circumstances. Please—won't you let me bring her to you? I'm sure that one look at her would change your attitude completely——'

'My attitude,' he interrupted harshly, drawing himself to his full, impressive height, 'is entirely my own affair, as is the way I conduct my relationship with my daughter or any other female, Miss Armitage.'

Lost to all propriety for the moment, Carey put up her chin, staring up at him in defiance. In for a penny, in for a pound, she thought recklessly. 'My sole interest, I assure you, is in the relationship you have, or rather *don't* have, with your baby daughter, Mr Savage. I do my best to make up to her for the lack of mother-love in her life, but you're her *father*. You should be doing something constructive about it. I'm just someone paid to take care of her, and while I love her very much . . .' She stopped mid-sentence, suddenly conscious of what she was saying. Oh, lord, it was true. She did love Alice—far more than was wise for a mere nanny. The discovery damped down her indignation as she realised she'd gone much too far, overstepping by miles the line drawn between employer and employee.

'Well, well,' drawled Patrick Savage, his head on one side as his bright eyes bored into hers. 'What a passionate creature you are, after all, Nanny dear. Not nearly so self-contained as you'd have people believe.'

'I apologise,' said Carey, mortified, her eyes falling. 'I had no right to say all that.'

'On the contrary. I found it very illuminating. The switch from Mary Poppins to Pollyanna was deeply impressive. Shall you count your attempted conversion of wicked father as your good deed for the day?' Patrick Savage possessed a voice of great charm, but for the moment the latter was overlaid by mockery so abrasive it set Carey's teeth on edge. 'Give up, Carey Armitage,' he went on with weary cynicism. 'I'm a hopeless case. I'm afraid fatherhood, instead of greatness, alas, was thrust on me. Babies possess no appeal at all as far as I'm concerned—particularly,' he added, wincing at the sound of Alice's distress, 'when they yell all the bloody time.'

'She does *not* cry all the time——' Carey checked herself hurriedly. What on earth was she doing? 'Alice,' she said with care, 'is merely using the only form of communication open to her at this stage. I apologise for my outburst, Mr Savage. Now if you'll excuse me I'll go and relieve Dilys. I'm afraid I was wet when I came in so she took over in order for me to change.'

'You were soaked to the skin.' The black eyes gleamed suddenly at the recollection, running over her again with such deliberate intimacy that colour rushed to Carey's cheeks as she hurried away towards the kitchen, certain that the mocking black gaze was following her all the way.

She found Dilys walking up and down the big kitchen, trying to hush an inconsolable Alice. Her face lit with relief when she saw Carey. 'She wouldn't take her juice from me, love. Knows I'm an amateur, I expect—no children of my own, see.'

'Neither have I, Dilys!' Carey laughed shakily as she took the distraught little bundle in her arms and cuddled the baby close. 'There, there, honey-bun, you didn't like being rushed home like that, did you? Did I frighten you, darling? I'm sorry.' She rocked the baby against her shoulder, crooning to her until Alice quietened, then took the bottle Dilys handed over and offered it to the baby, who discovered a drink was just what she needed after all the crying, and peace reigned.

'Magic!' said Dilys admiringly, and went back to her preparations for the evening meal. 'She knows you already, doesn't she?' Her round, kind face shadowed. 'Not surprising, mind. You're the nearest thing to a mother she's got, after all.'

Carey felt a yearning tenderness as she looked down at the moist, flushed little face against her breast. 'Yes, I suppose I am, poor little scrap,' she agreed quietly, feeling depressed. What a fool she'd been to sound off at Patrick Savage like that. It had done no good at all except to inform him of her own rash emotions where his daughter was concerned. Emotions she had no right to, and which she must learn to control before they got out of hand. One day, as was only natural, she and Alice would have to part with each other, so it was pointless to give full rein to her love for the child. Or for Alice to get too attached to her nanny. That way would lead only to heartbreak for both of them. And heartbreak, thought Carey bleakly, was not something to be recommended, as she knew only too well.

After the fiery little encounter of the afternoon Carey was unsurprised to receive a message from Patrick, via Dilys when she brought down his dinner tray.

'Mr Patrick is asking if you'll go up and see him, love. I'll listen for the baby.'

'Did he say what he wanted?' asked Carey with foreboding.

'No, *cariad*.' Dilys smiled wickedly. 'He was *very* polite, mind. Said you were only to go if you weren't busy.'

Convinced Patrick Savage meant to dispense with her services, Carey nevertheless insisted on helping a protesting Dilys clear up as she normally did, and forty minutes or so elapsed before she finally climbed the forbidden spiral stair, managing a smile at her own description. The Gothic atmosphere of the place was beginning to get to her! She took in a deep breath, then tapped on the massive study door and opened it in response to his summons.

He rose to greet her from one of the armchairs by the fireplace, a smile of such warmth and welcome on his tanned face that Carey felt stunned. 'I thought you weren't coming,' he said, waving her to the other chair.

'I always help clear away,' she explained.

He frowned. 'Why, for heaven's sake? That side of things is nothing to do with you.'

'I know. But I can't just sit and look on while Dilys does it all.'

They looked at each other in silence for a moment. Patrick was in the clothes of the afternoon, but Carey had taken time to change her dress and tidy her hair as some kind of support to face the reprimand she felt sure was the very least Patrick Savage had in store for her.

Patrick got up and went over to a table containing a coffee tray and silver salver of bottles. 'Coffee? Or a drink?' he asked.

'I'd love some coffee,' said Carey, relaxing very slightly. He didn't *sound* as though he was about to sack her.

'I keep all the makings for that up here,' he said, filling two cups from a coffee machine. 'I drink the stuff all day—in the hope that the caffeine will stimulate the mental processes. Today it hasn't worked at all. Cream? Sugar?'

Carey accepted both. 'Thank you.' She eyed him uncertainly. 'Was there something you wanted to say to me, Mr Savage—about Alice, or—or anything?'

He heaved a great sigh as he sat down. 'I think we said all there was to say on that subject this afternoon, don't you?' The corners of his mouth turned down expressively. 'You stated your case pretty emphatically.'

She flushed. 'I know. I was rude. I'm sorry.'

'Not at all! You were absolutely right about my— my attitude towards the child. I admit it freely. I just wanted you to understand that for the moment it's beyond me to do a thing about it.' A look of bleak torment flashed in the dark eyes, hidden quickly as he drank some coffee. 'If I tell you my real reason for asking you up here it's more than possible you'll turn tail and run,' he added lightly.

Carey's lashes dropped like shutters to hide her trepidation. 'What is the reason?' she asked.

'Would you find it hard to swallow that I just need someone to talk to?' he said with sudden vehemence, then shrugged moodily. 'To put it in a nutshell, Miss Carey Armitage, I suddenly grew sick and tired of my self-imposed isolation, on top of which I'm suffering from writer's block and haven't written a single damn word today I can use. Crazy, isn't it? My own book, blast it! I fought tooth and nail for the rights to do the teleplay myself, yet today you'd think I was writing it in my own blood!'

Carey smiled, inwardly limp with relief. 'Oh, I see.'

'Do you? Do *you* feel lonely sometimes, too?'

'Of course I do. Everyone does, Mr Savage.'

He sat staring at her, somehow managing to look graceful even when slumped in his chair on the point of his spine with his long legs sprawled in front of him. 'Do you think you could possibly bring yourself to say "Patrick"?' he said irritably.

She shook her head. 'Not at all suitable, under the circumstances.'

'Do you know,' he said conversationally, 'I hate that bloody word.'

'"Suitable"?' said Carey, startled.

'No. "Circumstances". It seems to crop up all the time, lately.' He gave a mirthless bark of laughter. 'Some of my characters have even taken to using it.' The black eyes narrowed. 'That reminds me. Have you by any chance read *Privileged Class*, Carey?'

'Yes.' She hesitated, then smiled rather shyly. 'I read it last year when it first came out, then when I got the job here I thought it would be a good thing to read it again, so I bought the paperback.'

He smiled warmly, looking pleased. 'Well done! Tell me—what do you think of it?'

Carey thought carefully before answering. Patrick sat on the edge of his chair, looking rather tense as he waited for her comments. 'I think it's a brilliant study in relationships,' she began, but he interrupted her impatiently.

'Never mind all that. Did you enjoy it as a story?'

'Oh, yes,' she said without hesitation. 'It's utterly absorbing from start to finish, only...'

'Only what?' he prompted.

'It's so bitter and disillusioned in places. Most of the characters display such—such inhumanity sometimes. The bitterness runs right through it.' Carey looked at him warily. 'Perhaps that's not what you wanted to hear.'

Patrick shook his head. 'On the contrary, it's exactly what I wanted to hear. A truthful opinion.' He grinned, looking disarmingly boyish. 'Most people—excluding the critics, of course—tell me what they *think* I want to hear.' He snapped his fingers suddenly. 'By the way, while I remember— part of my reason for asking you up here was that my mother rang again earlier. She sent her regards and hopes life at Llynglas isn't too trying, and thanks you for your letter. Writing's painful for her these days, so she'll ring you soon for a chat—about the child.'

'Thank you,' said Carey shortly, her hackles rising involuntarily at his use of the word 'child'. 'I'll look forward to that.'

'More coffee?' said Patrick.

'Yes. Thank you—but I can help myself...'

'No. Up here you're my guest, Carey.' He sprang to his feet and took her cup over to the table to refill it. 'Have a brandy with it?'

'No, thank you. I very rarely drink.' She smiled across at him with sudden humour. 'A tippling nanny has a touch too much of the Dickensian about it, wouldn't you say?'

He laughed as he sat down again, nursing a large glass of brandy. 'I find it difficult to think of you as "Nanny", anyway, Carey. To me they're elderly tyrants with starched bosoms who force children to eat up their vegetables and mind their manners.'

'Did you have a nanny like that, Mr Savage?' she asked, amused.

'Good lord, no.' His smile was reminiscent. 'I believe there was a young girl at home when I was young. The sort who ran after me and did the ironing and so on, but my mother actually took care of me herself.'

'Things are very different these days,' Carey told him. 'Lots of women enjoy fulfilling careers without depriving their children of one scrap of mother-love or security.'

'Very possibly.' The tanned face wore a with-drawn, morose expression as Patrick Savage swallowed half the brandy in his glass, and Carey finished her coffee, deciding it was time to go.

She hesitated for a moment, then decided to take advantage of his mellowed mood. 'Mr Savage, before I go, could I ask you something, please?'

The black eyes swivelled in her direction suspiciously. 'You may ask, by all means. I don't promise to answer.'

Carey's eyes filled with entreaty. 'I know you feel very strongly on the subject, but even at the risk of offending you, Mr Savage, I can't let this opportunity pass without asking again if it isn't possible for you to change your mind about—about seeing your baby? She's so beautiful, I'm sure if you just took one look at her——'

Patrick Savage jumped to his feet, overturning his glass with a crash of splintering crystal. 'What the hell does it take to convince you, Carey Armitage? Didn't I make myself plain this afternoon? I pay you to look after the child, not dictate to me as to my behaviour. The child is here in this house because there's nowhere else for her to go, not because I want her here. Frankly I don't see why my mother couldn't have you both with *her*— there's room enough in that flat of hers. Think of the fun you could have swapping stories about your employers with all the other nannies in the square!' His eyes glittered derisively. 'Unfortunately my lady mother flatly refuses to entertain the idea. Too old and too infirm, she tells me—which is a load of hogwash. She's got some bee in her bonnet about propinquity with the child winning me over in the end—Little Lord Fauntleroy and all that.'

Carey got up quickly, her face burning. No wonder he wrote so well on the subject of inhumanity! It came as second nature to him. 'I'm sorry,' she said coldly. 'I won't mention it again. As you say, I'm paid for looking after your daughter, not to express opinions. Please accept my apologies. I'll go back to my room now. Goodnight, Mr Savage.'

The broad shoulders slumped suddenly, and Patrick looked at her with such a dull, hopeless look in his eyes that all Carey's anger and indignation drained away.

'I'm sorry, too,' he said, in a flat, uninflected voice. 'I didn't mean to shout at you. But I meant what I said. I—I just can't face her yet. Call it unnatural, call it what you like, but it's something I just can't do.' He gave an apologetic shrug. 'I apologise for the snide bit about nannies. Heaven knows I'd be sunk without you, wouldn't I? If you really took umbrage and shook the dust of Llynglas from your sensible little shoes this minute I'd be right up the creek—my lord, you won't, will you?' he added, as though the truth of it hit home suddenly.

'No, Mr Savage. Not if you wish me to stay. I feel far too much responsibility towards Alice to do that. Goodnight.' Carey gave Patrick Savage an unsmiling, courteous little nod, then left him to his own company, which, by the look on his face as she closed the door behind her, augured badly for the night ahead of him.

CHAPTER THREE

AFTER the stormy passage in the study Carey fully
expected Patrick Savage to avoid her like the plague,
but she was wrong. He kept well away when she
was with the baby, it was true, but on her own she
began to run into him so often in the hall or in the
courtyard she wondered sometimes if he lay in wait
for her to appear. Their exchanges, brief and formal
at first, always ended with an enquiry from Patrick
about his daughter, as if he wished to make plain
to Carey that Alice was the primary reason for the
encounters. Carey, elated by any interest Patrick
took in his baby, however slight, took great care to
respond politely and pleasantly, to follow his lead
when he seemed disposed to linger, hoping against
hope that sooner or later he might capitulate and
ask to see his child. But he never did.

As June gave way to July the weather became
settled and hot and Dilys suggested that during
Alice's afternoon nap Carey spent an hour on the
stretch of beach which edged the lakeside bound-
aries of the house. The shingle shelved too steeply
to take Alice there in her pram, so while Dilys listened for the baby Carey yielded to the lure of the
sun and took a book and a rug to the tiny beach,
only to find she had company shortly after she
settled to read.

She scrambled to her feet in embarrassment at the sound of Patrick Savage's footsteps crunching on the pebbles, but he waved her back to her rug, apologising for his intrusion, and hunkered down beside her for a while, chatting idly as he spun pebbles across the water. After only a few minutes he left her again, telling her to make use of the little beach whenever she wished, and Carey watched his tall, slim figure stroll away, frowning. Was she imagining the fact that, unwilling though he might be to make friends with his little daughter, he felt rather differently towards Alice's nanny?

According to Dilys, sunny weather was not to be taken for granted in that part of the world. Carey needed no urging to make the most of it, and Patrick took to joining her for a few minutes, sometimes half an hour or so, every day.

'Must top up the tan,' he said lightly, on the second occasion. 'That's if you don't mind, of course?'

'Not in the least,' she answered with perfect truth, and smiled. 'It's your beach!'

'Nevertheless I'll leave you in peace if you prefer,' he assured her, and began spinning pebbles over the water with concentration.

'Dilys says the weather's not often like this at Llynglas,' said Carey elliptically, and he grinned.

'Very true—a sin to waste it.'

As time went by he lingered longer, until one day Carey was the first to make a move.

'Do you have to go?' he asked, as she began gathering up the rug.

'Yes, Mr Savage, I do.'

'Meaning I should get back to the grindstone, too, I take it!'

'Is the screenplay coming along better now?' she asked as they reached the gate in the wall.

'In relation to a certain day not so long ago, yes,' he said, avoiding her eye.

'Good.' Carey smiled at him cheerfully, then went across the courtyard and into the kitchen, where Alice was just showing signs of waking up from her nap.

'Hello, honeybun,' said Carey, picking her up out of the pram. 'Have you been a good girl?'

'Good as gold,' said Dilys, making tea. 'There's brown you are, *cariad*. Like something off those holiday posters.'

'Living at Llynglas is almost like a holiday in a way,' said Carey, as she gave the baby a drink. 'It's beautiful enough, certainly.'

'Too quiet for a girl like you—and holiday-makers don't look after babies day and night.'

Carey laughed, scolding the housekeeper gently, assuring her that few babies were better behaved than her sweet little Alice, and a quiet life was a good thing.

'In moderation maybe, girl, but you've hardly been outside the place since you got here.'

'I'll go to Welshpool on Friday,' Carey promised. 'I need some suntan lotion, of all things, and you're away for the day on Saturday, aren't you?'

Dilys looked doubtful. 'I don't know that I should go, not with Mr Patrick here.'

Carey cuddled the baby against her shoulder, frowning over the little head at Dilys. 'Nonsense.

You can leave cold food, if it makes you any happier. Please go, Dilys. Your mother must be missing you.'

With some reluctance Dilys agreed it could be managed. But, she said firmly, Mr Patrick would have to collect his own trays. Carey was in Llynglas to look after Alice, not Alice's father. 'If you can call him a father,' concluded Dilys with a sniff. 'I suppose he can't bear to look at the poor little soul because of his wife, but it isn't fair. It's not Alice's fault she's in the world, is it? It's his!'

Carey found herself looking forward rather eagerly to the sessions of debate and discussion on the beach with Patrick Savage each day. Sometimes he appeared on the beach almost as soon as she did, which was no miracle, of course, since he looked down on it from his vantage-point in the tower. But on Patrick's part there was no attempt to disguise the fact that he enjoyed Carey's company, and, much against her will, she was flattered. He was, she reminded herself constantly, merely lonely and starved of conversation, since the only other human being he ever laid eyes on was Dilys, who regarded him very much as the master, a being above such things as idle conversation. Whatever his reasons were for seeking her out, Carey found herself counting the minutes each day until it was time to be with Patrick, who, in ragged denim cut-offs and a pair of dark glasses, looked as though he'd just abandoned a surfboard rather than the keyboard of a word processor.

Carey, who felt obliged to keep to nothing more revealing than a sleeveless dress for her sunbathing sessions, eyed Patrick's bare, muscular torso askance when he made his first appearance in such casual style.

'Something amiss?' he enquired.

'No,' she said quickly, flushing as she turned away to gaze out over the water.

'You've got that disapproving-Nanny look on your face,' he told her, and Carey laughed, embarrassment forgotten, as Patrick changed the subject to the problem he was wrestling with over a section of dialogue between the main protagonists in his screenplay, and soon she was offering suggestions, hesitant at first, then bolder as Patrick paid them due attention. Although he was frank enough to dismiss some straight off, he fastened on to one angle between hero and heroine with such enthusiasm that he went dashing off to his keyboard at once with the aim of getting it down on disc, and Carey watched him go rather ruefully, sorry in one way that her chance remark had cost her Patrick's company, yet at the same time highly gratified to be taken up on her suggestion. Next day he was back to report on the success of her idea.

'Perhaps you should collaborate with me on my next book,' he said as he sat beside her, long, bare legs crossed yoga-style as he leaned over to see what she was reading.

'Afraid not,' said Carey in a stifled voice, aghast to find that his warm proximity took her breath away. 'I'm a reader, not a writer.'

'And of arcane detective fiction by the look of it!' He laughed. 'I see you've been raiding my late uncle's thriller collection.'

'I adore them,' she said brightly. 'Ngaio Marsh, Dorothy L. Sayers—and Margery Allingham particularly. I've nourished a secret passion for her Albert Campion from the age of twelve.'

Patrick bent to peer into her averted face. 'Any other secret passions?' he asked softly, then straightened, alarmed at her stricken look. 'Hey—what did I say? Don't you feel well?'

'Too much sun,' said Carey, scrambling to her feet, folding her rug with hands which shook. She managed a smile for Patrick as he uncoiled himself to hand the book up to her. 'I'd better go in now. Goodbye, Mr Savage.'

'See you tomorrow, perhaps,' he said slowly, his eyes fixed on her face as he walked with her to the wooden gate in the wall.

Carey nodded animatedly. 'Probably—if the weather holds up. It's been marvellous lately, hasn't it? Apparently it's hotter here than in the South of France at the moment. Dilys says it won't last, of course...' She trailed into silence as she saw the question in his eyes, then turned tail and fled, terrified he might read her mind. The last thing she wanted was for Patrick to discover he had the power to evoke feelings she had truly believed were the sole copyright of the man who'd awakened her to those feelings in the first place. And for hours through a long, sleepless night she lay tossing and turning, racked by illogical pangs of guilt over her infidelity.

The next day Carey woke to rain. There would be no question of any session on the beach, and she was glad. Of course she was glad. Patrick Savage might be a lonely, attractive man who was grieving for a dead wife but, more importantly, he was also an employer who paid her good money to look after his daughter. Her reaction to his—his personal charm was purely because she was vulnerable just now, she told herself firmly. He was a dangerously attractive man. She'd do well to remember it in future and preserve a well-defined distance between herself and anyone who not only paid her wages but trusted her to look after his child. Consequently, instead of enjoying the daily interlude with Patrick Savage on his private beach, Carey, bedevilled by her own restlessness, took his daughter for a long walk in the rain. She was out so long that when she finally got back Dilys flew at her in relief, clucking over her like a mother hen.

'Just look at you, girl,' she scolded. 'You'll catch your death—your jacket is sodden.'

'I'm fine, Dilys, really,' said Carey, laughing as she stripped off her windbreaker. 'I didn't realise I'd gone so far. By the time I turned round it seemed like miles back to Llynglas.' She bent to take out Alice, who was demanding a drink in no uncertain tones. 'All right, all right, young lady. Dilys has your juice all ready.'

'Let me give it to her,' offered Dilys, but Carey shook her head.

'I'd better give her the drink, then you can play with her while I change.'

'I know, I know. She likes you to feed her,' agreed Dilys ruefully, and busied herself with making a fresh pot of tea. 'Mr Patrick wanted to know where you'd got to, by the way.'

Carey kept her eyes on Alice, who was sucking in her fruit juice with gusto. 'He knows I'm back. He was watching from his window as I came over the causeway.'

'Afraid you'd lost your way, I expect.'

'I could hardly do that. There's only one road.'

Dilys set a place of fresh, warm Welshcakes on the table beside the teacups. 'That's as maybe, but when the mist comes down you can stray on to the moor, or down into a ditch before you can say knife, *cariad*.'

Carey pulled a face. 'In which case I'll stick to the gardens or the main road in future. I went along the other one for a change because I thought there'd be less traffic. I get a bit bored with wheeling the pram round the gardens every day.'

'It must be a bit boring here altogether, love, for a pretty girl like you,' commented Dilys, pouring herself some tea.

Carey shook her head, smiling. 'Not a bit of it! I like the peace and quiet here. I read a lot and I'm provided with my own television, remember. And tomorrow I'm going to buy some material and make myself another dress.'

Carey saw nothing of Patrick that day, except for a brief glimpse of him at the tower window. She had pretended not to see, uncertain how to acknowledge him. A cheery little wave might have looked too familiar, she'd felt, and after the first startled glance Carey had kept her head down and had hurried inside to Dilys. To her consternation, after only a day without talking to Patrick she found she missed him. Which, she informed herself, was ludicrous. Surely by now she'd learned her lesson when it came to men. After the pain and misery of her first and only essay into love it was to be hoped she had more sense than to lay herself open to that exquisitely painful torture ever again.

It was bad enough, she thought unhappily, to love Alice so much. It would be sheer lunacy to develop a *tendre* for the father as well, however slight. In future she would take steps to keep well out of Patrick's—and harm's—way.

As a step in the right direction Carey kept to her plan next day and left Alice in the willing hands of Dilys, plus Megan Pugh, mother of two, in able support. Looking forward to her little break, Carey set out to catch the mid-morning bus outside the gates of Llynglas, her sights set on lunch and a little shopping amid the pleasing mixture of half-timbered and Georgian architecture in the prosperous market town of Welshpool.

It was, she found, rather pleasant after all to spend time away from Llynglas, and she indulged happily in some window-shopping as she dodged between the showers of a day more like April than July. Carey bought her suntan cream with a wry smile, wondering if she'd have any more occasion to use it now that the weather had broken, afterwards spending so long in a bookshop she had to rush over choosing a dress length and a remnant of silk to fit in lunch before catching the bus back to Llynglas.

'Carry your bags, lady,' drawled a familiar voice as Carey emerged from the shop. She stared in surprise as a grinning Patrick Savage, dressed in scuffed leather jacket and Levis, his bare brown feet in familiar leather loafers, casually relieved her of her packages.

'Why, hello!' she said, secretly shaken by delight at the sight of him. 'I didn't expect to see you here.'

Patrick took her arm, hurrying her along the pavement as the heavens threatened to open up again. 'Needed stamps and so on,' he said laconically. 'Dilys said you were in town. Had lunch yet?'

'No——'

'Good. Neither have I.' Patrick steered her across the road towards the Royal Oak, a brick-built hostelry which had plainly served the town for a century or two.

Carey eyed it in alarm. 'Oh, but I didn't mean——'

He paused on the pavement outside the hotel. 'Are you saying you don't want to lunch with me?'

She frowned. 'Yes—I mean, no...'

At which point the rain came down like lead rods and put an end to the argument. Patrick grasped Carey firmly by the elbow and marched her into the Royal Oak and straight into the dining-room, giving her no time to admire the beautiful staircase in the reception area as they passed, and since they were immediately shown to a table further protests seemed futile.

'This is very kind of you,' she said stiffly, after they'd chosen from the interesting menu.

'Don't sound so surprised,' he said mockingly. 'I'm not all bad, you know.'

'Few people are, Mr Savage,' she agreed.

He sighed. 'Couldn't you possibly bring yourself to call me Patrick?'

Carey shook her head positively. 'As I've said before, in our particular circumstances it's not suitable.'

He leaned forward, scowling. 'I swear I'll howl like a dog if I hear that word much more. My mother says it with every other breath—she rang this morning, by the way,' he added, leaning back in his chair again. 'Said she'd ring back tonight for a word with you, and gave me a very generous piece of her mind when I admitted that, as far as I know, this was the first time off you'd had since your arrival.'

'My fault entirely,' said Carey quickly.

'*You* know that. *I* know that. My mother, however, is unshakeable in her belief that the fault is mine!'

Patrick's face was full of such soulful injury that Carey gave him a sudden, involuntary smile, her eyes brimming with laughter.

He blinked, his face suddenly blank. 'Glory!' he breathed. 'Why don't you smile like that more often?'

Suddenly Carey felt strangely light-hearted. 'Oh, I do,' she assured him blithely. 'It's just that you haven't seen me do it before.'

'How right you are! Chance, as they say, would be a fine thing, Miss Carey Armitage.' He broke off as his choice of ox heart in Marsala sauce was placed before him, and they were halfway through lunch before he returned to the attack. 'Is there any reason,' he persisted, 'why nannies can't be on friendly terms with *parents* as well as babies? Queen Victoria passed away a long time ago, you know.'

Carey looked up from her gougons of sole thoughtfully. 'I suppose not, Mr Savage.'

Patrick pounced. 'Ah! But friendly terms call for first names, Carey.'

'You're perfectly at liberty to use mine,' she assured him, and sat back in her chair. 'That was delicious. Thank you.'

'Don't change the subject. Why won't you call me Patrick?' he demanded wrathfully.

Because, thought Carey with regret, that way lies danger. 'Dilys calls you *Mr* Patrick. Perhaps——'

'No!' he said forcibly, then gave her a determined, glinting smile. 'I'll get my own way in the end, you know.'

'It's not good for someone to get their own way all the time.'

'I know, Nanny. It's not good at all—but it's great fun!'

Patrick Savage in cajoling mood was hard to resist, and Carey laughed as she let herself be persuaded to eat a sinful, cream-laden pudding, followed by several cups of coffee as they argued enjoyably over differing opinions on the latest bestselling thriller Carey had bought. They emerged later into sunshine with such a transient look about it that Patrick hurried Carey back to the Porsche before the gathering clouds rolled any nearer.

'Thank you for my lunch. It was very kind of you,' she said, once they were on the road back to Llynglas.

'On the contrary. It was very selfish. I wanted your company so I more or less forced myself on you.'

Carey glanced at him quickly, but his eyes were fixed on the road, his profile giving nothing away. 'Why?' she asked.

'Why did I force myself on you?'

'No. Why did you want my company today?'

'Because I missed you badly yesterday, Carey. I cursed the rain. And when I saw you coming back from your walk I envied the—the baby.'

Carey stared unseeingly at the road curving ahead of her through the hills which ringed Llynglas. Patrick took one long brown hand from the wheel and touched it for a moment to hers, which was clutching the seatbelt as though it were a life-raft. She tensed, sitting bolt upright in her seat. 'The scenery along here is utterly breathtaking, isn't it?' she said brightly.

'Oh, utterly! And the weather's *so* much more like spring than summer today, wouldn't you say?'

Whereupon Carey lapsed into silence, which lasted until the Porsche was gliding along the narrow carriageway towards the lake. As Patrick brought the car to a halt in the courtyard Carey bent to gather up her packages.

'Thank you for driving me home,' she said with a polite little smile.

'My pleasure.' He jumped out of the car and strode round to help her out. 'Just say the word and I'll drive you to *and* from Welshpool next time.'

Carey shook her head, looking up at him steadily. 'I think not, Mr Savage.'

At her deliberate formality the light died in his eyes in the way Carey was coming to know by this time. 'You mean it wouldn't be correct for Nanny to be seen jaunting off with "the master"!'

'More or less. Thanks again.' And Carey went off towards the kitchen, leaving him looking after her with a wry, bitter twist to his mouth.

Dilys was pacing up and down the kitchen, a protesting Alice in her arms. The housekeeper's round face flooded with relief at the sight of Carey. 'You're back!' she said thankfully as Carey dumped her packages on the table so she could take Alice.

'Oh, Dilys. Has she been a naughty girl?'

The baby snuggled against Carey, her cries dying away to snuffling noises of content as the longed-for arms cuddled her close, the familiar scent of Carey's hair and skin reassuring her with their aura of love and security.

'Just look at that,' said Dilys, shaking her head in wonder. 'Would you believe it?'

'Has she given you a hard time?' asked Carey, her throat thickening as she rocked the baby lovingly.

'No, no. It's just the last half-hour. Megan had to catch the early bus, because she's off on holiday tomorrow, see. So I took Alice for a walk, but I had to turn back because it rained cats and dogs, and ever since then the baby's been very restless.'

Dilys smiled ruefully. 'If you ask me she was missing *you*, love. I just wouldn't do. Look at her—she's practically asleep already.'

'Which is entirely the wrong time to choose,' said Carey, joggling the baby. 'Hey there, honeybun. Wake up. It's bathtime now.' She smiled down at the drowsy baby, stroking her cheek, and Alice opened her eyes and smiled back with such innocent trust that Carey's heart turned over.

Dilys cleared her throat, sniffing. 'Did you ever see such a smile—you mean the world to that child, Carey.'

Which, thought Carey later as she put Alice to bed, augured badly for further outings to Welshpool, alone or otherwise. She sighed as she thought of Patrick's offer to drive her there. A good thing she'd already said no to such dangerous delights. Even if the idea had been feasible, Alice's objections to her nanny's absence put a very effective damper on it. On the other hand, thought Carey, troubled, it wouldn't do for poor little Alice to get too reliant on just one person either—whoever the person was. If Dilys felt up to coping with Nanny's time off, Nanny would do well to make herself go off at regular intervals so Alice could get used to more than just the one person in her life. Nanny would have to get used to it too, Carey reminded herself bitterly. One day an attractive man like Patrick Savage would inevitably marry again and provide Alice with a new mother, a thought which stabbed Carey to the heart with a two-edged blade.

Over dinner Dilys spent most of the time giving instructions about the food she'd left in readiness in larder and refrigerator. Mr Patrick, it seemed, would come down to fetch his trays at one and seven o'clock respectively.

'Said could you keep the baby out of the way at those times?' said Dilys uncomfortably, avoiding Carey's eye.

'Don't worry,' Carey assured her. 'I'll get the food ready, then make myself scarce as well. Before you go, tell him to leave the trays outside his door when he's finished with them and I'll collect them so quietly he'll never know I'm there.'

Dilys sighed unhappily. 'Best I don't go at all, really.'

'Of course you must go! You'd make me feel terrible if you didn't.'

'It's Mam's birthday, see, love, and there's only me left to be with her now. The neighbours are very good, of course, but——'

'Dilys, stop *worrying*.' Carey jumped up and went over to the carrier-bag she'd left on the dresser. 'This was meant for you, but since it's your mother's birthday, would you like to give it to her instead, as a little gift from me?'

Dilys's face glowed as she regarded the impressive box of chocolates. 'There's nice of you,' she said, sniffing. 'Mam'll be ever so pleased. Eighty tomorrow, but with a terrible sweet tooth. I'll be lucky if I get one of these!' She got up and gave Carey a hug. 'And don't worry, Wayne Evans from Llanfach Farm will get me home tomorrow night. I may be a bit late, mind.'

'Stay as late as you like, woman!'

During the evening Mrs Savage rang to speak to Carey about Alice's progress. 'And how about you, my dear?' she asked after a while. 'How are you coping with life at that extraordinary folly of a place?'

Carey was able to say with complete truth that she enjoyed the quiet of Llynglas very much.

'And Patrick?' Mrs Savage's tone was acid. 'In our exchanges so far I gather the wretched boy refuses even to look at his daughter.'

'I'm afraid so, Mrs Savage.' Carey hesitated. 'On the other hand I fancy he won't have much choice in the matter as Alice gets older. Babies rather tend to make their presence felt.'

'Carey, take my advice and allow her to be as obtrusive as possible. He can't hide away from her forever—regrettably rude though he was when I pointed this out to him earlier.'

Carey smiled to herself, able to imagine the exchange with no trouble at all, and assured Mrs Savage that her son would no doubt reconcile himself to fatherhood in time.

'Until which happy day all we can do is hope,' said Mrs Savage with irony, and ended the conversation by assurances of her own support at any time should Carey need it.

Carey could have done with it next day, if only to get Dilys off the premises. The housekeeper felt so guilty about leaving Carey alone at Llynglas that it took a lot of hard talking and an escort along the causeway with the baby in the pram to make sure Dilys finally got on the bus to Llanfach.

In some ways Carey rather enjoyed being alone in the big, stone-flagged kitchen when she got back. She fed the baby her lunch at noon, then put her down for her nap in the perambulator in the kitchen instead of her cot, an arrangement which seemed to meet with Alice's full approval, since she went off to sleep quite happily while Carey guiltily indulged herself with the sandwiches Dilys scorned as a proper meal. Before she ate, Carey put ready-scrubbed potatoes to boil, then afterwards she assembled cold chicken and salad on a tray, along with crusty rolls, a dish of butter and a jug of dressing. Following instructions, she added a sprig of mint and a knob of butter to the hot potatoes, put them in a lidded dish on the tray and covered the entire thing with one of Dilys's gleaming white cloths before beating a hasty retreat with the pram before Patrick Savage could come down for his lunch and surprise them.

The day was fine and sunny, with no threat of rain or mist, so because the gardens were open to the public Carey took the mountain road again. She pushed energetically, reflecting that this was entirely the wrong time for a walk while Alice was sleeping peacefully. The afternoon outing was normally reserved for the period when the baby was wakeful, to pass the time between afternoon rest and bathtime. Now routine would be disrupted. Which, thought Carey cheerfully, was totally unimportant alongside the pleasure old Mrs Howells would take in having Dilys at home for her birthday.

Carey stayed out on her walk as long as she possibly could. When she got back the tray had been returned to the kitchen table, dishes washed, and a note propped up against them.

'Thank you for my lunch. Don't worry about dinner. I'll forage for myself later when the coast is clear. Patrick.'

By which he meant after the baby was in bed, thought Carey, resigned. As foreseen, the afternoon proved trying. Once Alice was awake she made it plain she expected to go out in her pram again, and in the end Carey gave in, afraid the noise would disturb Patrick in his tower. Come home Dilys, she thought ruefully, as she trundled the heavy perambulator over the causeway again.

Carey felt tired and thoroughly out of sorts by the time she got back, and Alice seemed tuned in to her mood. Bathtime was normally something the baby enjoyed, but for once she was thoroughly fractious, grizzling and complaining throughout the entire procedure, then topped it off by throwing up her supper, crying pitifully all the time she was changed again, wringing Carey's heart. It was ages before Alice could be persuaded to drink a little boiled water, after which she became quiet at last as she lay exhausted against Carey's breast.

'About time, too,' Carey informed her, exhausted herself by this time. 'It's way past your bedtime, honeybun.'

When Alice was asleep in her cot at last, and looked as though she might stay that way for a while, Carey had a shower, put on navy linen trousers and a pink sweatshirt, tied up her damp

hair with a ribbon, then went down to the kitchen
to make herself some supper before Patrick Savage
took it in his head to do the same. Ten minutes
later, feeling ridiculously furtive, she went back up
to her room with a tray of cheese and salad and
fruit, plus a large pot of coffee, and switched on
her television at a low volume before subsiding in
a chair with a sigh of pleasure to eat her supper in
peace.

The peace lasted until nearly nine, when a knock
on the door brought Carey to her feet to answer it,
thinking it was Dilys back from her day out. When
she found Patrick outside on the landing Carey
stared at him in astonishment, pushing a strand of
slippery hair away from her eyes.

'Mr Savage! What is it? Couldn't you find
something?'

He looked tense, his face dark and strained above
his white shirt in the gloom of the landing. 'I'm
afraid I've got bad news——'

'David?' she gasped, going cold.

He scowled. 'No,' he said curtly. 'It's Dilys, not
one of your boyfriends. Her mother's had a heart
attack. Dilys sounded frantic over the phone, absolutely beside herself because she's left us in the
lurch, or so she feels, because Megan is on holiday
and Dilys can't leave the hospital.'

'Oh, poor Dilys,' said Carey with compassion.
'What a thing to happen. It was her mother's
birthday, too.'

'The root of the problem, I gather. There was
some kind of birthday tea with the neighbours. Too

much excitement for old Mrs Howells. Nice old girl, too.'

'The last thing Dilys need worry about is what's happening here,' said Carey firmly. 'She's left enough food for a siege anyway, and if the place doesn't look as spick and span as usual I'm sure you won't mind.'

'I don't care a damn.' He rubbed his chin absently. 'Anyway, it's you Dilys is worried about; afraid you'll take on too much in addition to—to your usual duties.'

At which point Miss Alice Savage gave voice to a loud reminder of Carey's 'usual duties', and Patrick stiffened, looking hunted. He muttered something unintelligible, then took off as fast as his long legs could carry him towards sanctuary in his tower.

Thoroughly put out, one way and another, Carey tried in vain to soothe the baby. A nappy change, a small quantity of milk, several lullabies and a lot more cuddling than usual failed signally to quiet the distressed Alice. In the end Carey took her down to the kitchen for some boiled water, walking up and down with her for a while before trying to administer the drink, whereupon Alice not only rejected the water but threw up the milk.

Carey cleaned them both up, changed the child again, sponged the hot little face then rocked the baby rhythmically against her shoulder, deeply worried by the alarming heat radiating from the small body. For once she wished passionately that they were less isolated at Llynglas. She wanted medical advice, and wanted it quickly, but the nearest doctor was in Llanfach, five miles away. For a moment she was tempted to ring up her brother in Cardiff, but dismissed the idea at once. No doctor would diagnose over the telephone.

Carey was forced to put the baby down while she rang the emergency number for the Llanfach medical practice. The duty doctor was out on call, but would come to Llynglas as soon as possible, she was informed. In which case, Carey decided militantly, Alice's father had better know about it whether he wanted to or not. She picked up the baby, hushing her as she rocked her against her shoulder.

'Quietly, my darling,' she murmured soothingly. 'Carey's got you. But I've got to put you down for a moment because I must talk to your father——'

'Can't you keep that confounded child quiet?' grated an irate voice from the doorway, and Carey swung round, her arms tightening protectively about the distraught baby. Patrick Savage stayed where he was, plainly poised for flight, and Carey lost her temper.

'No, I can't keep her quiet!' she flamed. 'She *is* a baby, you know, and babies cry when there's something wrong.' She fought for calm as she looked down at the flushed little face. 'She's feverish. Her temperature's soaring higher by the minute so I took it on myself to call the doctor.'

Patrick advanced into the kitchen slowly, his eyes on the baby's head against Carey's shoulder. 'When's he coming?' he asked in a constricted voice.

'As soon as possible. He's out on a call.' Carey looked up, her eyes widening as she saw the look of blank astonishment on his face. 'What is it?' she cried, alarmed.

'She—she's got blonde hair.' He went on staring, as though having taken his first look at his baby daughter he couldn't tear his eyes away.

'Full marks for observation,' snapped Carey, then blushed painfully. 'I'm sorry,' she said swiftly. 'I'm a bit edgy. She doesn't normally cry like this, you see.'

And suddenly the baby quietened, giving little exhausted hiccups as her sobs died down.

'What's wrong?' demanded Patrick wildly. 'Is she worse?'

'No. Just tired out.' Carey shifted the baby higher on her shoulder, and Alice Savage opened her eyes and looked straight up at her father for a moment, gave a quivering little sigh and closed them again, nuzzling her head against Carey like a little animal seeking comfort.

Carey looked up to surprise a very strange look indeed on Patrick Savage's face. 'What is it? What's the matter?'

He raked an unsteady hand through his hair, still staring down at the baby as though he'd never seen one before. 'She—she's got *dark* eyes, Carey—like me.'

Carey nodded, smoothing a gentle finger over the damp, silver-gilt rings of hair on the baby's forehead. 'Her hair's like yours too. She's beautiful, isn't she?'

Patrick nodded, for once quite plainly bereft of speech.

Carey eyed him for a moment, then decided to strike while the iron was hot. 'Would you like to hold her?'

Patrick shied away like a startled horse. 'No!'

Carey shrugged. 'Just as you like. There, there, honeybun,' she said soothingly as the baby's face crumpled. 'Don't start crying again, sweetheart. The doctor will give you some medicine and you'll soon feel better.'

'I thought babies always had blue eyes,' said Patrick faintly, like a man in shock.

'Alice probably did at first, but by the time I made her acquaintance they were already nearly as dark as they are now. She's the image of you,' Carey added firmly.

He propped himself against the table, legs stretched out in front of him, looking from the baby to Carey in a way which might have seemed comically sheepish in any other man, she decided. On that dark, tanned face the look of apology was irresistible in its appeal.

'You know, I couldn't bring myself to look at her because I was certain she'd be exactly like her mother. Ice-blue eyes, red hair...'

'Yes, I know, I've seen your wife on television,' said Carey very gently. 'But in actual fact babies rarely look *exactly* like either parent. Alice is something of an exception. Her resemblance to you is pretty startling in one so young.'

At which point Alice began to cry again, heart-rending sobs which drove her father demented.

'Carey, for Pete's sake—can't you *do* something?' he said in anguish.

'I'm afraid to give her anything else until the doctor gets here,' said Carey unhappily, too taken up with trying to soothe the child to spare attention for the fact that the father was prowling round the room in a fever of anxiety which would have been highly interesting at any other time.

The sound of a car outside in the courtyard came as an enormous relief to them both, and sent Patrick tearing to the outer door to open it to a young man with rugby-forward shoulders and a sensible manner which lowered the tension in the kitchen immediately.

'Mr Savage?' he enquired. 'Geraint John from Llanfach. I gather there's something wrong with this young lady.' He smiled at them in cheerful reassurance, then examined the baby, and in a very short time diagnosed Alice's trouble as chicken-pox.

'Chicken-pox, Doctor?' Carey's face blanched.

'Where the hell could she have caught chicken-pox?' asked Patrick blankly. 'Besides, aren't babies under six months immune from things like that?'

'Not always, unfortunately, Mr Savage.' The doctor took a small bottle of medicine from his bag and handed it to Patrick, then shook hands with him, brushing aside thanks for coming so far out of his way on a Saturday night. 'All part of the job,' he said briskly. 'Give her plenty of fluids, don't worry if she doesn't fancy eating for a bit, Mrs Savage. I'll be back tomorrow to see how she is.'

After he'd gone Carey racked her brains to solve the mystery of how Alice could possibly have contracted chicken-pox. Then she remembered the children hanging over the pram a few days earlier in the gardens. Any one of them could have been the culprit.

'It's my fault,' she blurted, as Patrick returned from seeing the doctor off.

'How do you make that out?'

'There were children in the gardens the other day when I came through with the pram. They came over to look at the baby while I stopped to chat with Gwilym Davies. I should never have let them.'

Patrick shook his head impatiently. 'You can't protect the child from everything, Carey. Don't blame yourself, please.' He touched her hand. 'Besides, the doc said it'll probably be a mild case.'

'You don't understand——' began Carey, then checked herself hurriedly.

His eyes narrowed. 'I might if you explain.'

'I meant that because Alice was premature I'm probably more inclined to worry. Quite unnecessarily, I'm sure,' she added, praying fervently that she was right.

'Can I help?' he asked, as he walked with her towards the stairs.

'Not really.' Carey glanced down at the flushed little face against her shoulder. 'Now she's had her dose I hope she'll sleep for a bit—for her sake, not mine.'

'I'm well aware of that,' Patrick assured her, rubbing a weary hand over his chin as he looked at his daughter's sleeping face. 'Carey—I'm deeply grateful to you for caring so much about my child.'

'Thank you, Mr Savage,' she said, choking back the tears as she turned to climb the stairs with her little burden. Patrick laid a hand on her arm to detain her, and Carey turned, her face on a level with his as she paused on the first stair.

'I want you to know something else, too,' he said, looking at her very steadily. 'I've been an out-and-out fool, I know. About this little scrap, I mean. Lord knows what I thought the sight of her would do to me, yet until tonight I hadn't the guts to bring myself to find out. It's not something I'm proud of. My lady mother was absolutely right, as usual. One look at Miss Elinor Alice Savage *was* enough, after all. Not to turn me into a doting father overnight, perhaps, but at least enough to show me what an utter lunatic I've been in every other way as far as she's concerned.'

CHAPTER FOUR

THE next week was worse than anything Carey had previously experienced as a nanny. Poor little Alice was desperately unwell for a while, and one or other of the doctors from the Llanfach practice called to see her once, sometimes twice, every day. Dilys was utterly distraught when she rang to report on her mother, quite plainly torn in two when she learned how things were at Llynglas.

'I told her not to worry about it,' said Patrick, who abandoned all pretence of trying to write, and took to haunting Carey's room most of the time to monitor his daughter's progress. The contrast between his former and his present attitude would have amused Carey at any other time. As it was she had no attention to spare for anything or anyone but Alice, except to be glad of someone to share the responsibility, also of Patrick's unexpected skill in the kitchen. The situation was reversed with a vengeance. It was Patrick, now, who ran about with trays, since Carey flatly refused to leave Alice other than to take a swift shower twice a day, or to load the washing-machine downstairs, at which times Patrick never stirred from his daughter's side. He moved the baby's cot into Carey's room at her request, and from then on Carey never left the room for more than a few minutes at a time.

'Thank heaven for disposable nappies,' she said with a sigh one day.

Patrick looked at her anxiously. 'Carey, you look terrible.'

'I'll be all right when I've had some sleep.' She gave him a tired smile, and went over to look at Alice, who was less restless than usual but about to wake any minute by the look of her.

'And when will that be?' he demanded as he joined her. 'Look, Carey, why don't you sleep in the other room tonight—I'll stay here with the baby?'

Carey smiled at him, touched. 'Thank you, but no. I wouldn't sleep, and then two of us would be awake all night. Can't have the chef too tired to make dinner!'

Patrick smiled. 'OK, Nanny.' His eyes grew sombre as Alice began to cry weakly. 'Poor little scrap, she sounds exhausted.'

Carey lifted out the baby and began to change her, smoothing calamine lotion on her pock-marks, which, to Carey's deep relief, were fewer than anticipated, and mainly on the baby's chest, where Alice's flailing fingers couldn't get at them to scratch. They were fading already, she noted with joy, and turned starry eyes in Patrick's direction.

'I think she's finally on the mend!'

It was an opinion endorsed by Dr John later that evening. Carey had set him right by this time about her status in the household, and after a careful examination of the baby he nodded his head.

'I think we're out of the wood, Miss Armitage. No danger of encephalitis now. Alice will soon be right as rain, you have my word.'

Carey smiled at him shakily, while Patrick's eyebrows shot into his hair.

'Encephalitis?' he said, horrified. 'What the hell is that?'

'Inflammation of the brain,' replied the young doctor matter-of-factly. 'It's pretty rare, but a risk we can't overlook when so young a baby contracts chicken-pox. Little Alice here is in no danger now, I promise, Mr Savage.'

After Patrick had escorted the doctor downstairs Carey laid Alice back in her cot then hung over her, limp with reaction as she gazed down at the tiny sleeping face.

'You knew all along,' said Patrick accusingly as he stalked back into the room, a white line around his mouth as his eyes glittered darkly into hers. 'You never said a word about encephalitis.'

She shook her head, trying to smile. 'I asked the doctors to keep quiet about it. I thought ignorance would—would be b-bliss...' Her voice faltered, and a sudden sob shook her. She spread her hands in apology as tears streamed down her face. 'I'm so sorry——'

'Sorry?' Patrick pulled her into his arms and held her head against his chest as if she were Alice, stroking her hair as her control, curbed so long on a tight rein, disintegrated completely. 'Good lord, Carey, you've no reason to be sorry. You've been an angel and I'll always be in your debt. I'm bloody

glad I didn't know what the possibilities were—I'd
have gone off my head!'

His voice cracked at the last and Carey threw her
own arms round him, her urge to console as in-
stinctive as his. They stood holding each other for
a long, quiet interval, until something indefinably
different crept into the embrace at last, and Carey
pushed herself away, mopping at her swollen eyes
with the handful of tissues Patrick handed her. 'I'd
better get myself together before I start Alice off
again,' she said thickly, avoiding his eyes. 'She
needs sleep.'

'So, dear Nanny, do you,' said Patrick, clearing
his throat. 'Tonight I'll sit up with my daughter.'

'No——'

'Yes,' he interrupted, then swung round as a
tactful cough sounded out in the hall. 'Who the
hell——?' He strode to the door to find Dilys out
on the landing looking embarrassed.

'I called but I couldn't make you hear,' she said,
her round face creased with worry as Carey flew to
her and embraced her fervently. 'How's that poor
little soul, *cariad*?'

'She's better, thank heavens. Oh, Dilys, how
wonderful to see you! How's your mother?'

'Well enough to be left now—in the hospital, of
course. I'm back,' she added, and Patrick gave a
choked laugh.

'And are we pleased to see you! I'll run you in
to visit your mother twice a day every day, if you
like, if it means you can take over.'

'Not a moment too soon by the look of the place,'
she said tartly, her face softening as she went over

to look at the baby. 'Poor little mite,' she whispered, then tiptoed out of the room with the light of battle in her eyes as she made for the kitchen.

'My fault, Dilys,' Patrick assured her as he went after her. 'Carey hasn't set foot outside the bedroom except to see to the laundry. I'm to blame—for everything.'

It was some days later before Carey felt things were back to normal and Alice truly on the mend. She found it hard to relax until the baby was eating and sleeping quite well again. But, as Alice's cheeks began to resume their former roundness at last, Carey found her own looks beginning to improve after longer periods of sleep and fresh air, plus the tempting meals Dilys produced with such magnificent disregard for calories.

Patrick had duly returned to his writing in the tower-room, but he emerged from it every night to eat a dinner he insisted Carey share with him in the dining-room on the ground floor of the tower. No further reference was made to the embrace, but neither was there any attempt to return to the way things had been before Alice's illness, since Patrick threatened dire consequences if Carey made any move to reinstate the nanny-employer relationship she'd once tried so hard to maintain. The crisis of Alice's illness had forged a durable link between herself and Patrick Savage, Carey admitted secretly. It was futile to deny that she derived a dangerously addictive pleasure from dining with him each night, particularly when Patrick Savage set himself out to be a witty, charming companion who made it plain he enjoyed Carey's company. Yet it was his attitude towards his tiny daughter which thrilled and delighted Carey even more than his undisguised interest in herself. It was impossible, sometimes, to remember that once she'd been obliged to keep Alice tucked away out of his sight. Since the illness Patrick had to be restrained from picking Alice up out of her pram on every possible occasion, even when she should have been left there to sleep, and Carey, amused, was forced to resort to what he called nanny-tactics to discipline him.

'Your daughter will quickly get out of hand if you carry on like this,' she warned him.

'I know,' he said, unrepentant. 'But when you consider what a blithering idiot I was about her before, do you wonder I feel such an urge to make it up to her now?'

When the telephone rang during dinner a week or so later Patrick returned to the dining-room, dour-faced, to say someone called David wanted to speak to Carey. Her eyes lit up as she flew from the room to make her apologies to her brother and Jenny and explain why nothing had been heard from her for a while. When she got back to Patrick he was peeling an apple with such ferocity that Carey felt for it.

'Who,' he asked, his eyes on his task, 'is David?'

'My brother. With all the trouble over Alice I haven't written to David and Jenny lately. They were worried.'

Patrick looked up with a quick, seraphic smile reminiscent of his daughter's as he offered her half his apple. 'Tell them they can visit you any time.'

'Why, thank you,' said Carey, touched. 'I will. I'd like that.'

'It must be boring for you here, day after day.'

'Not in the least. I love Llynglas.'

'My wife wouldn't set foot in the place,' Patrick said suddenly. 'She said she only felt alive in the city.'

Carey, taken by surprise, said nothing for a moment, uncertain whether to offer any comment or not. 'Perhaps,' she said slowly, 'she was one of those people who find quiet and solitude intimidating.'

His mouth twisted. 'That was it exactly, of course. Stephanie was used to bright lights and television studios. She starred in a successful soap for years, of course, which provided her with the perfect excuse for staying put in town. Did you ever see it?'

'Once or twice.'

'Not your kind of thing, I imagine,' he said drily.

'It wasn't that—just that it went out fairly early in the evening. I rarely had time to myself until later.'

'Very tactful. It was far too banal for someone of Stephanie's talent.' He shrugged. 'She was always talking about leaving it to return to the stage, but the money was so good she could never bring herself to have her character written out. She didn't fancy being killed off, as she put it.' His face set in bitter lines.

Carey poured coffee in silence, wary of trespassing in an area where Patrick Savage still plainly suffered pain.

'What a restful companion you are, Carey,' he commented after a while, leaning back in one of the balloon-back chairs ranged around the massive Victorian dining table.

'When I was young I was a chatterbox,' Carey told him, hoping to lighten his mood. 'My parents never tired of saying how worried they were because I was late learning to talk, then how bitterly sorry they were once I'd mastered the art.'

'What exactly was it, I wonder, that quietened you down so much later on in life?' he asked curiously.

'Maturity, hopefully!' Carey stood up as Dilys came in to clear away. 'I'd better check on Alice.'

'Sleeping peacefully a few minutes ago,' the housekeeper assured her.

'I think I'll pop upstairs just the same,' said Carey, who had qualms about leaving the baby for any length of time since the illness. She smiled at Patrick. 'I'll say goodnight, then.'

'Hang on,' he said, getting up. 'Dilys, could you sit in Carey's room for a bit, and watch *her* television for a change, to keep tabs on Alice? I need to sort a few things out in the study—on the subject of my daughter,' he added, as Carey looked at him questioningly.

'Of course, Mr Patrick.' Dilys beamed at Carey. 'You go up to her now, love, and I'll be with you after I've put this lot in the machine.'

Her own consent, thought Carey as she left the room, appeared to be taken for granted.

'I hope you'll forgive the encroachment into your spare time,' said Patrick when she joined him later in the study.

'If it's to talk about Alice I can hardly complain,' said Carey, who these days no longer addressed her employer as 'Mr Savage'. But since she couldn't bring herself to say Patrick, either, she solved the problem by avoiding any direct form of address at all.

'Have a drink,' said Patrick, looking oddly tense as he waved her to a chair.

Carey eyed him uneasily. 'No, thanks.'

'Nanny talking, I suppose.'

'Not really.' She smiled ruefully. 'To be honest, my alcohol threshold is abnormally low. One glass of wine acts like three in my case.'

He grinned disarmingly. 'Ah! I see now why you stick to Welsh water at dinner. How about coffee, then?'

'Lovely.'

Patrick seemed to find it vital to keep up a flow of conversation as he filled cups and poured himself a modest brandy, going on at some length about the Theophilus Savage who'd fulfilled a boyhood dream by building a castle for himself. 'Fortunately,' he told her, 'the nurseries my late uncle set up here a few years ago are so popular the sale of plants and the entrance fees more or less keep the gardens going with the present staff. This place, of course,' with a wave of his hand, 'is my responsibility. I'm always threatening to sell it, but my mother won't hear of it. She wouldn't dream of living here herself, but she hates the thought of it going out of the family.'

'I can sympathise with her on that,' said Carey.

'What about me?' Patrick shot at her suddenly, his black gaze impaling hers as he shook the bright hair back from his forehead. 'Do you feel sympathy for me?'

Carey put down her cup carefully, forcing herself to look away. 'Yes,' she said at last. 'I would, I trust, feel sympathy for anyone I knew in your present—situation,' she said hastily, remembering his dislike of the word 'circumstances'.

'How temperately you express yourself, Miss Armitage!'

The silence which followed his remark was in no way uncomfortable. Carey usually felt tired at this time of day, and it was very pleasing to relax in a comfortable chair in this beautiful, romantic room, where the Gothic windows framed different pictures of sunset on water, or twilight on woodland, according to location. It was no penance at all to sit there quietly, content that Alice was in good hands, and she lay back in her chair, relaxed, until Patrick's next remark changed the mood completely.

'Carey, what happens to Alice when you have to leave her one day, as sure as hell you will?' His eyes met hers in such fierce question she felt pinned to the back of the chair.

'It—it depends,' she said guardedly.

'On what?'

'At what stage that particular occasion arises, how old she is, whether she's in school——'

'It still won't alter the fact that one day the woman she regards as her mother won't be around any more.' He rose to his feet with a sudden restless movement. 'I've thought about this incessantly lately—ever since Alice was so ill, and I saw for myself how totally she depends on you.'

'You were there, too,' Carey reminded him.

'I was only the back-up, Carey. You're the one who matters to her, the one she wants all the time. And one day you won't *be* there.' Patrick sat down again, looking at her challengingly, as though waiting for her to provide some solution to the problem. 'I can't stop thinking about it,' he said, pacing up and down. He gave her a mirthless smile. 'I know what you must be thinking. It's only a short time since I looked on the child as an encumbrance in my life. Then bingo—I take one look at her and immediately she's a person, a little girl. *My* little girl. And how the hell does a man bring up a daughter single-handed?'

Carey smiled reassuringly. 'Simple. You marry again. Provide Alice with a mother.'

His lashes dropped over the bright black eyes, the fine skin of his eyelids paler, Carey noted, than the rest of that darkly-tanned face. When they rose again his expression was sardonic.

'Very neat. All I have to do, then, is find some accommodating lady not only willing to mother my child, but to bury herself here with her for months at a time while I write. Because that is what I do. And this place is where I do it best.'

'Don't you own a house in London?' asked Carey quietly.

A shadow dulled his expressive face. 'Not any more. I sold it after—after Stephanie died.'

'Couldn't you buy another, or a flat, a *pied-à-terre* in town, and have the best of both worlds?'

'If I did, is there any guarantee that the lucky lady of my choice would desert it periodically to immure herself behind my ruined walls?'

Carey could think of nothing else to suggest. Also, she thought, looking at him speculatively, she had an idea he knew perfectly well what he meant to do, and was merely putting his problem into words, rather than actually seeking help with it.

'Well?' he demanded after a while. 'No more bright ideas?'

She shook her head. 'Not really. If the prospect of marrying again is unlikely——'

'Oh, I didn't say that,' he interrupted quickly. 'Tell me, Carey. Why were you so positively negative when I asked about *your* matrimonial intentions?'

Carey tensed. She looked away quickly, unwilling to meet the intent black scrutiny. 'I don't intend to marry for the simple reason that the only man I ever wanted wasn't—isn't—free.'

Patrick let out a deep breath. 'I thought it might be something like that.' He leaned across and took one of her hands in his, holding it lightly as though afraid she might snatch it away. He looked deep into her eyes, with a warmth and compassion she would never have believed him capable of in her first encounter with him. 'Did the guy feel the same about you?'

Carey nodded, unable to answer for the lump in her throat.

Patrick went on holding her hand, giving her time to recover. 'Will his situation ever change? I mean, he's not a priest, or something?'

She gave him a wry little smile. 'Goodness, no. He's married, that's all.'

'No possibility of a divorce.'

'None whatsoever.'

'But Carey, you're young. There are other men in the world. Are you sure you won't find some other man to love one day?'

She drew her hand away gently, smiling at him with a shaky brilliance which made him blink. 'Nothing's sure in this world, is it? But in this case it's highly unlikely.'

'So you're going to stay single, making do with other people's families all your life, until one day you'll find yourself old and grey and all alone, Carey.'

She shivered, her blood icing over in her veins at the prospect, even as she managed a smile. 'That's right. I'm quite happy to spend my life looking after other people's babies. So if you're content that I make a satisfactory nanny for Alice you don't have to worry. I'll stay with her as long as you want me to stay.'

Patrick Savage shook his head sombrely. 'Bloody waste, you know. You're a good-looking lady, Carey Armitage, with a brain behind those beautiful grey eyes. You're a bit too restrained and contained for your own good, but at least I'm beginning to understand why. Crossed in love, no less.'

Carey jumped to her feet in sudden panic. 'I'll say goodnight now——'

'I'm sorry, Carey.' Patrick sprang to put a restraining hand on her shoulder and Carey froze, appalled to find that it burned like a brand. Dear lord, she thought wildly, what kind of woman am I?

'Sit down again,' said Patrick, eyeing her searchingly. 'Please. I still haven't got to the subject I asked you here to discuss.'

She shot a pointed look at the clock. 'Would you be fairly quick, then, please? I should be getting back to relieve Dilys.'

Patrick pushed her back into her chair and stood over her. 'All right, Miss Carey Armitage, listen carefully and don't interrupt, no matter what, OK? Not until I've said my piece.'

'Very well.'

'Let me put things as succinctly as possible. Fact one—I am a widower with a small baby. Fact two—you are a lady who loves babies but seems dead sure she will never marry and produce one of her own. Fact three——' He hesitated, then shrugged irritably. 'Why beat about the bush any longer? The simple fact is, Carey Armitage, that I want to marry you.'

'No!' Carey blurted and jumped to her feet, ready to run, but he caught her at the door.

'For heaven's sake, girl, I said *marry*, not ravish.' He held her by the shoulders, looking down at her with such urgency she stayed still under his hands.

'Look. Alice needs a mother, Carey, but—oh, hell, how can I put it? Let's just say I'm not in need of a wife exactly. Not in the usual way, at least. After Stephanie I don't want the normal kind of marriage. You say you don't want a husband either, so if you agreed to marry me all you'd get would be a grateful companion and security for life, and Alice would keep the only mother she's ever known.'

Carey trembled under the restraining hands, and Patrick let her go. 'I can't believe you'll never want a wife—on the usual terms, I mean,' she said, her colour rising.

'Why?'

'Because you're a very attractive man and you must meet hundreds of beautiful women in the course of your life——'

'Carey, haven't you been listening? I don't *want* the sort of wife who'll expect a glittering social life and a husband ready to dance attendance on her. That, loosely speaking, was what I had before, and it causes problems. When I write I'm shut up on my own sometimes fourteen hours a day and when I've finished I'm so bone-weary all I want to do is sleep—alone. And *my* favourite form of diversion these days is standing up to my thighs in a river for hours on end after salmon—not women.' He shrugged, his eyes wearily mocking. 'At the risk of offending your delicate sensibilities, Miss Armitage, I think I should make it clear that the trauma of my wife's death has put a decided damper on my libidinous tendencies. Only keep it under your hat, there's a good girl. Bad for P. Savage's image. Once upon a time, as we writers say, I used to enjoy rather a different kind of reputation.'

'I'd heard,' said Carey primly.

'That was before I married Stephanie. She—she changed my life in many ways. After Stephanie nothing's quite the same.'

Carey's eyes lit with sympathy as she gazed up into his bleak face. 'I know how you must feel. My case is not dissimilar. The man I love isn't dead, of course, but he might just as well be as far as I'm concerned.'

He reached out a hand to touch her hair. 'Poor Carey.'

She moved away deliberately. 'Please. I don't need pity.'

'I know. Don't be so prickly!' His eyes softened cajolingly. 'But won't you let me take care of you, Carey? I've been very lucky with my career. If I never write another word I can still keep you and Alice in reasonable comfort for the rest of your lives, you know.'

'I'm not concerned with the financial aspect——' she began wretchedly.

'The other aspects of matrimony needn't worry you either,' he interrupted, deliberately blunt. 'Your bed will be your own, Carey—should you consent, that is. All I'm asking is a civilised arrangement between two sensible people.' He grinned suddenly. 'Now I've probably scuppered myself completely. Doesn't sound very attractive put like that, does it?'

Carey's answering smile was wry. 'To most women, I suppose not. It takes a little getting used to, of course. Marriage—of any kind—is something I'd long ago dismissed as out of the question as far as I'm concerned.'

'Have I changed your mind?' he said swiftly, a glimmer of triumph in his eyes as he pounced on a slight thawing in Carey's attitude.

'I don't know,' she said slowly. 'The idea's too new for me to take it in properly.'

'Will you at least promise to think about it?' Patrick glanced across at his desk. 'Tomorrow I go to London to deliver the first half of the script, and argue like hell about it for a few days. That gives you until Saturday to make up your mind.'

'All right,' said Carey. She gave him a thoughtful look. 'What happens if I say no?'

'Nothing. We go on as we are and hope time will solve Alice's problem in some other way.' Patrick put a long brown finger under her chin to raise her face to his. 'When I come back I'll ask just once what decision you've made, and whatever you say I'll take as final. Coaxing, persuasion and so on are things I'm good at—I'm used to having my own way, I warn you. But on this I'm prepared to abide by whatever you decide. Because I like you a lot, Carey, and I admire and respect you too. It's my considered opinion that we'd do well together. Do you agree?'

'Since it's not a question *I've* ever considered, I don't know,' she answered, determined to be honest. 'Your proposition—or proposal, if you like—comes as a bit of a shock. I hadn't the faintest idea what you had in mind when I came up here tonight.'

'No, I know,' he agreed. 'That's what makes you rather different from most women of my acquaintance.'

'The fact that I'm your child's nanny makes me very different, for a start, Mr——' Carey stopped at the look on his face.

'For heaven's sake, whatever relationship we have from now on, can't you bring yourself to say Patrick?' He took her by the shoulders and shook her very gently. 'Go on. Say my name. I won't let you go until you do.'

Feeling incredibly silly, Carey muttered, 'Patrick, then,' very crossly, and won a delighted laugh as a reward.

'You're embarrassed!' he chortled, then relented, and opened the door for her. 'All right, Carey, I'll let you go now—and try not to look so pleased to escape!'

Her eyes danced. 'I think it's that door of yours. It reminds me of the convent where I went to school. We had to wait outside Mother Superior's door if we misbehaved—she was never angry, just horribly hurt. Sheer agony!' She frowned at the look on his face. 'What have I said? Is something wrong?'

Patrick looked down at her thoughtfully. 'Are you a Catholic, Carey?'

'No. The convent was the best girls' school where I grew up, that's all.' Her eyes narrowed. 'Ah! If I had been it might have made a difference, I suppose—regarding the offer of marriage.'

He shook his head. 'No. Not in the least. My view of marriage, difficult though you may find it to believe, has always been the ''death us do part'' kind. If you *do* decide to marry me, Carey, I'd better make it clear from the start that the arrangement would not only be civilised, but for Alice's sake I'd expect it to be permanent.'

CHAPTER FIVE

IN SOME ways it was a long, long week before Patrick's return to Llynglas. Yet in others Carey felt it was far too short to make what was likely to be the most momentous decision of her life. She yearned to discuss it with someone, to seek a disinterested opinion, but, like the other major problem in her life not so long before, she knew only too well she had to cope with it by herself. And since Alice had now reverted to being a happy, healthy baby, sleeping sometimes from early evening to seven or so in the morning, Carey had no lack of time to herself to think things through.

She had been tempted by Patrick's startling proposal from the very first. His remarks about growing old and grey alone returned to haunt her again and again, changing her mind every time she made up her mind to refuse. And in some ways, she admitted, she had no desire to refuse, if it meant living at Llynglas, or even having Patrick Savage as that *rara avis*: a husband who was an interesting and friendly companion but would make no physical demands on her. It was, she thought honestly, useless to deny Patrick Savage's physical attraction, or her own response to it. Nevertheless, the sexual side of marriage was an area she had long ago vowed was out of the question with any man except the one man in the world with the power to melt her bones and turn her blood to fire. Carey shied away from the thought, horrified to find that her pulse still raced and her breath grew laboured at the thought of his kisses even now, after all this time. She sighed. Marriage to Patrick—or at least the platonic form of it he had in mind—might well prove to be the antidote to that particular lacerating pain.

Carey spent a lot of time at her window each evening when Alice was asleep, her fingers busy with the piece of silk she was smocking to make a tiny dress, her brain working overtime as the sun sank into the veil of mist above the lake. And one evening, a day earlier than expected, she saw the Porsche come gliding over the causeway through the golden haze and knew that crunch-time was at hand.

'You look tired,' was Patrick's blunt comment as Carey went running down the stairs to greet him. 'Alice playing up?'

'No.' She smiled as she took the hand he held out. 'She's been as good as gold.'

Patrick looked fine-drawn himself, his face weary above the formal shirt and tie. He tugged off the latter, telling her the bags under his eyes were the product of too many late nights and far too much argument. 'But I won most of it,' he said smugly, steering her towards the kitchen, 'and I'm starving. I haven't had any dinner.'

Carey peered in the refrigerator. 'There's a large pie in here. Would you like a wedge? I can heat it up for you.'

'Don't bother. If it's Dilys's famous meat and potato pie I'll eat it as it is.' Patrick's eyes never left her face as she cut bread and laid a place at the table. 'Now then, let's not beat about the bush. I came early because, Miss Armitage, difficult though you may find it to believe, I was anxious to know what you've decided. *Have* you decided?' he demanded, as she set a plate in front of him.

'Yes,' said Carey briefly, finding that now Patrick Savage was actually here with her again her indecision had vanished. 'If you still want to marry me, I accept.'

Patrick jumped to his feet and seized both her hands in his, his eyes blazing with gratitude. 'Thank you, Carey. I'll never give you cause to regret it, I promise.'

'There's just one proviso,' she said quickly.

Patrick's eyes narrowed. 'Yes?'

'If, some time in the future, you meet someone you want as a more normal sort of wife—someone you can love as much as you loved Stephanie, I mean—I'd release you at once if you wanted a divorce.' Carey's eyes fell as Patrick's eyebrow rose quizzically.

'Does that mean you require me to reciprocate, Carey?'

'No,' she said, turning away quickly at the sudden, illuminating realisation that this was the last thing she wanted. 'In my case the situation will never arise.'

Patrick touched her cheek lightly. 'I find myself growing more and more curious about this ''case'' of yours, Miss Armitage—no,' as she dodged away,

'I won't tread on any susceptibilities.' He pushed her down in a chair at the table. 'Now, sit there and talk to me while I eat. Tell me what's been happening at Llynglas while my back was turned.'

Carey asked mock-humble permission to make coffee first, and Patrick laughed, plainly delighted she felt able to tease him, then listened attentively while Carey gave him a blow-by-blow account of his daughter's progress. In return he told her about his fight to keep his script more or less as he wanted it, then snapped his fingers suddenly. 'I almost forgot—my mother sent her regards, Carey, and told me to say well done.'

Carey felt puzzled. 'Very nice of her, but what exactly am I supposed to have done?'

'Transformed me into the doting father she says she knew all along I would be, given time. She was utterly unbearable with her "I told you so" routine.'

'It was Alice who waved the wand, not me, Patrick.' His eyebrows rose, and Carey eyed him, frowning. 'It's true,' she insisted.

'I was merely thinking how good it was to hear you say "Patrick" so naturally.' He gave an odd little laugh. 'It convinces me, I think, that you actually mean what you say.'

'It should,' said Carey briskly. 'I always mean what I say.'

'A woman above rubies!' He helped himself to more coffee, smiling at her. 'Few women are virtuous in that particular area, in my experience.'

'Then I'll come as a nice change, won't I?' she said, suddenly light-hearted.

'That you will, Carey Armitage, believe me!' Patrick jumped up, holding out his hand. 'Let's go and take a look at my daughter, then I vote we go for a walk. If we keep to the garden below Madam's window we'll hear her if she cries.'

'All right.'

Now Patrick was back with her again Carey let herself admit how much she'd missed him, finding it it very pleasing indeed to stroll in the garden with the tall man whose face showed dark in the twilight under flaxen hair which needed cutting badly, something she now felt entitled to point out.

'Good lord,' he said, chuckling, 'you sound like a wife already!'

'Sorry—didn't mean to nag.'

'Oh, I like it! It's a long time since anyone cared a damn what I looked like, Carey.'

She looked away quickly to hide a surge of compassion.

'Now what's going on in that neat, glossy head of yours, I wonder,' he remarked, as they reached the rose arbour directly beneath Alice's window. 'Let's sit down for a while and enjoy the peace and quiet.' He yawned a little. 'Hellish drive tonight— the motorway was packed.'

They sat in companionable silence for a while on the rustic bench, Carey feeling unexpectedly happy now the die was cast. Although she'd burnt her boats now she found she had no regrets over accepting Patrick's proposal—and felt oddly touched at his pleasure. Somehow she'd never expected him to display such overt gratitude. Alice's future had quite obviously been troubling him far more than he'd ever admitted, and rightly so. Any man in his situation would feel the same, she told herself firmly, left with sole responsibility for a small, motherless baby daughter.

'When will you marry me?' asked Patrick without warning.

Carey gazed at him, startled. 'I—I don't know. Not yet awhile. Christmas, perhaps?'

'Christmas!' He turned to face her, frowning blackly. 'Why wait until then?'

Carey's face grew warm. 'I—I assumed you'd want a suitable period of mourning to elapse.'

The familiar shutter dropped in his eyes. 'Oh. I see. I took it you needed time to steel yourself for the ordeal.'

'Of course not. After all,' she pointed out, 'it won't make any difference to the way we are now, will it, except for an official document?'

'Heaven rest us, what a practical creature you are!' he mocked, then sighed. 'I suppose you feel I'll get a bad press for marrying too soon after Stephanie's death.'

Carey winced at his bluntness, uncertain how to answer him.

'I think it's time you heard the true story about Stephanie,' said Patrick slowly, the pain very apparent in his attractive drawl. 'Our marriage was—well, a viable partnership, but only because it was agreed we should each pursue our lives in our own particular way. Make no mistake, there were no liaisons with other people on either side. But our marriage changed inexorably as time went on. For one thing Stephanie was ten years older than me.

When we got married I'd just had my first play produced in the provinces, and I was the dazzled and adoring rookie, she was the established star. I don't know when we began to grow apart— probably as I grew more mature, and Stephanie more conscious of her age. Then towards the end she became almost paranoid about making our marriage "complete", as she put it. She had some crazy idea about producing a prodigy with her looks and my brain, and ultimately she died because she set her heart on a pregnancy her gynaecologist warned would be fatal for her.' Patrick stared into the distance with sombre eyes. 'If she'd agreed to adopt she'd still be alive today. I was dead against such a foolhardy attempt at her time of life, but in the end Stephanie tricked me into doing what she wanted.' He gave a short, mirthless laugh. 'When Stephanie played seductress no man could have held out against her—which doesn't stop me feeling as guilty as hell, or change the fact that my one fleeting lapse of self-control made her pregnant and ulti- mately killed her. Which is why I ran away to the Morgans' beach house and holed up there like a hermit after the baby's birth caused Stephanie's death, just as predicted. I felt like an assassin.'

Carey felt shaken. She put a hand on his arm. 'Please. You can't blame yourself. If Stephanie was so determined——'

Patrick turned his head to look down at her with bleak eyes. 'But I do blame myself, Carey. Don't you see? Because I no longer felt the same for her, Stephanie gambled her life away to have the child she was convinced would make everything right again. The months before the baby was born were the worst of my life. She was ill most of the time, and as she grew weaker my guilt got stronger and stronger until I could hardly live with it.'

Carey stared up into his face, which, even by the faint light of the new moon, had a despairing look about it which cut her to the heart. Her hand moved down to his and grasped it tightly.

'Don't go on, please,' she urged. 'You're making yourself ill!'

'No, I'm not, Carey. I've damn well made myself better,' he said fiercely, his hand bruising hers with its grip. 'I've never said anything of this to a living soul. It's like lancing a wound to let the poison out.' He twisted round suddenly and held Carey close, his arms almost cracking her ribs as his cheek moved over her hair restlessly. 'It's better you know the truth. I couldn't go on letting you think I'm in mourning in the usual, conventional way for Stephanie. Those last months caged up together were hell for us both. I begged her to have the pregnancy terminated, but Stephanie was determined to prove the doctors wrong. She scoffed at me. "Successful productions are my speciality, darling," she said, and refused to listen to the doctors—or to me. If she had she'd be alive today.'

Carey sat still within the impersonal ferocity of Patrick's embrace, and gradually his arms slackened, his lean, graceful body beginning to relax a little against her. She breathed in shakily, and put a hand up to his cheek. 'Is that why you kept away from Alice? Because you were afraid she'd look like Stephanie?'

He nodded. 'I was convinced the child would be the image of her—a constant reminder of my guilt. As if I needed one.'

'Whereas Alice has your black eyes and, I fancy, the nose you share with your mother,' said Carey, deliberately prosaic.

'Heaven help her, poor scrap,' he answered in a voice more like his own, and Carey let out the breath she'd been holding.

'She's the living image of you already, you know.'

'I do. You can't know what a relief that is to me, Carey. The moment I set eyes on Alice I felt as if some great load had rolled off my shoulders, that my life could return to something like normal.' His eyes sought hers in the dim light. 'It would be even better if I thought you were around to share it with me, Carey. Or does all this make you want to back out?'

'No—not in the slightest. I'm *glad* I know the truth.'

'Thank goodness for that!' He lifted one of her hands to his lips and kissed it, holding her eyes with his. 'And how about you? Would confession be good for *your* soul, too?'

Carey drew away a little. 'Patrick, don't be offended, but—but I don't think it would.'

He stood up, drawing her up with him. 'Whatever you say, Carey. But if ever you *do* want a shoulder to cry on, make sure it's mine, please.' He turned her face up to his and kissed her forehead as gently as though she were Alice. 'Now,' he said, with a deliberate change of mood. 'Let's fix a date for the wedding—and don't start talking about Christmas again,' he added, his voice cracking slightly.

Carey laughed, sliding her hand through the arm he held out to her as she entered into a good-natured debate, sensing his urgent need to return to normality after the dark disclosures of the past few minutes. Eventually it was decided the wedding would take place as soon as the television script was finished, but that it would remain their private secret until it was time to inform their nearest and dearest of the small and utterly private ceremony Carey felt suitable for the occasion.

'Unless, of course,' said Patrick, as they went into the house, 'I should ask your brother's permission. I will if you like, Carey.'

The idea quite appealed, she found. Unnecessary though it might be, it somehow added a touch of normality to a marriage that promised to be very different from the one joked about with her friends at the convent when she had been a schoolgirl. Then the general consensus of opinion had leaned to the tall, dark, impossibly handsome and utterly besotted for any bridegroom worthy of consideration. A bit different in actual fact, thought Carey, since she was about to join forces with a bridegroom who was tall and good-looking enough, but with hair the wrong colour and bent on a mother for his daughter rather than a wife for himself.

'I think I do like,' she said reflectively. 'Perhaps I might invite David and Jenny here for a weekend some time soon—when he's not on call, and you're not glued to your keyboard, that is.'

Patrick put out a hand and touched her cheek. 'Of course, Carey. Any time you say the word I'll be only too glad to meet your family. Could you possibly cope with Mother at the same time?'

Carey bit her lip, her grey eyes glittering, panic-stricken, as she stared up at him. 'I hadn't thought of that. Won't she disapprove of your marrying Alice's nanny?'

Patrick cast his eyes heavenwards. 'Why on earth should she? When I saw her yesterday all I could hear was how amazingly lucky I was to have you——'

'As a nanny, not a wife.'

Patrick grabbed her by the elbows and shook her ungently. 'If Mother's arthritis would allow, she'd probably be down on her knees with gratitude to know you're willing to take on Alice and me for life. I didn't like to jump the gun and let on that I'd asked you, but it was pretty clear to me that she approved of you very much in all ways—even said cryptic little things about it being a waste for a girl like you not to have a family of your own——' He stopped short, his face suddenly very austere. 'And she's right, of course,' he went on. 'It is a waste. Are you very sure about this, Carey? Am I ruining your chances of a normal marriage by coercing you into this one?'

Carey looked straight into his eyes. 'Before you proposed, Patrick Savage, I had given up all idea of ever marrying at all. Ever. So please don't worry on that count. I've had almost a week to think this over. I came to the conclusion I'm lucky to be of-

fered a future rather different from the old, grey
and lonely variety you mentioned not so long ago.'

Patrick winced. 'Did I really say that? Sheer
blackmail.'

'But horribly accurate,' said Carey, grimacing.
'It was no contest, really, considering the alternative you forecast.'

Patrick took both her hands in his. 'I repeat my
promise, Carey. I'll try never to give you cause to
regret your decision. But remember, if at any time
between now and the wedding you change your
mind, you're absolutely free to back out, and just
go on taking care of Alice in your present capacity.'

Carey was deeply touched. She looked up into
the dark, intent face above her, her eyes lambent
with sincerity as she shook her head. 'I've given
my word, Patrick. I won't back out.'

He raised both her hands to his lips with an air
of dedication. 'You're a girl in a million, Carey
Armitage. I pity the poor bloke who let you slip
through his fingers.'

Carey's lashes fell to veil her eyes. 'Please,
Patrick. If—if we *are* to enjoy a happy relationship
in future, it would be easier if you could forget there
was ever any other man in my life.'

Patrick bent, and for the first time touched his
mouth fleetingly to hers. 'Easier still,' he said very
softly, his eyes glittering as he drew back, 'if you
could too, Carey.'

Utterly incapable of answering, Carey gave him
a very wobbly smile then started up the stairs, but
halfway up she decided there was something she

had to say before she settled down to sleep that night. 'Patrick.'

He was still at the foot of the stairs, looking up at her. 'Yes, Carey?'

'I must ask you something,' she said with determination.

'Ask away.'

'After we're married are you still going to sleep in the tower?'

His stood very still, his eyes unreadable. 'I hadn't thought that far. Why? Would you prefer that I did?'

'No.' Carey fidgeted a little. 'What I'm trying to say is that I'd quite like Alice to grow up in a normal ambience, with parents as similar to other parents as possible.'

Patrick moved nearer, his graceful body taut as a bow. 'I'm not sure I understand what you have in mind, Carey.'

'I just thought you might like to take up residence in the old master bedroom next to Alice and me.'

All expression drained from his face. 'Yes,' he said without inflexion. 'Good idea.'

Carey eyed him uncertainly. 'I—I thought it might be better as far as Dilys is concerned, too.'

'Then it shall be done. Never let it be said I didn't bend over backwards to please Dilys!'

'Have—have I annoyed you in some way, Patrick?'

'No. Of course you haven't. But for future reference it might be better if you make yourself clear from the start.' Patrick gave her a wolfish grin. 'For a moment there I actually thought you were inviting me to share your bed.'

Carey's chin lifted. 'Of course not.'

The gleam in his eyes sent the blood rushing to her face. 'Is such an invitation beyond the bounds of possibility, then?'

'Yes,' she said coldly, ignoring a sudden leap of her pulse at the thought. 'Otherwise I would have rejected your proposal. Which,' she added with emphasis, 'I still may, if you have any misconceptions on the subject.'

'No, Carey.' He shrugged gracefully. 'As I said before, all I'm asking for is a civilised, companionable sort of marriage.'

She nodded briskly. 'Good. And I'm sorry if I misled you by talking about sleeping arrangements. Alice was my only motive for suggesting the three of us at least occupy the same part of the house. If you prefer to keep to your tower it's fine by me.'

Patrick shook his head. 'No, I think you're right. Ivory towers are cold, comfortless places to live in forever. Even for someone like me.' He gave her a wry smile. '*And* for someone like you, Carey Armitage.'

CHAPTER SIX

PATRICK SAVAGE'S suggestion had been a honeymoon in some exotic, lively spot as a change from the quiet of Llynglas, but Carey disagreed. For one thing, she pointed out practically, this was just a holiday, not a honeymoon, and for another she felt they ought to take Alice with them.

Patrick was not so besotted a father that this idea appealed in the slightest. Alice, he maintained, would be nine months old by the wedding day, and no longer in the slightest bit premature, nor, with luck, suffering from any childish ailment. In a word, he said firmly, she could perfectly well be left with someone else while her father took his new wife on a honeymoon, or holiday, or whatever description Carey preferred for the break Patrick felt they both thoroughly deserved. Carey, who found the word 'honeymoon' oddly unsettling anyway, was anxious to abandon the subject, particularly when Patrick pointed out that no matter how much time they spent together, which was nowhere near as much as he would have liked because of his rush to get the script finished, he was always conscious that at Llynglas Carey had one ear open for Alice. The honeymoon, he assured her, was going to be different.

Carey was still unhappy about leaving Alice behind. Who, she demanded, *was* going to take care of her while they were away? They could hire a nanny, Patrick retorted flippantly, and Carey ground her teeth and prepared for battle, but he spiked her guns by coming up with a surprise solution.

David and Jenny Armitage had duly brought young Paul to Llynglas for a weekend visit which had been pleasantly successful. Mrs Savage had made the effort and hired a car to drive her down from London, and the entire weekend had passed without a hitch. Patrick had, as intended, asked approval of the forthcoming marriage from Dr David Armitage, who, though slightly staggered at first, had been deeply pleased for his sister, while Jenny, utterly thrilled by the idea, had fallen madly in love with Alice, and had spent hours playing with both children.

'Jenny would love to take Alice,' said Patrick, looking pleased with himself. He grinned. 'And think of the advantages in the arrangement. If Alice gets ill again she'll have a doctor in the house!'

'That's not the point,' objected Carey. 'Jenny's a doctor's wife, remember, which is no sinecure, and she already has one very lively baby only a bit older than ours.' She flushed at the arrested look on Patrick's face. 'Well, you know what I mean. I tend to think of Alice as mine since—since things have changed. And I'm going to be her stepmother anyway.'

'I loathe the word stepmother. Besides, Carey, you know perfectly well that in every way but the biological fact you *are* Alice's mother, and no child could be blessed with a better one.' Patrick smiled at her across the dinner table, raising his glass to her in toast, and Carey glowed with a quick rush of pleasure.

'Thank you, kind sir.'

'And, to resume the argument, I thought it might be a good idea if Dilys went along with Alice to your brother's place. She likes Cardiff, and her mother's well enough to leave for a while. In fact, Dilys is dead keen—doesn't get away from this place much as a rule.'

'You mean you've asked her already,' said Carey, resigned.

'Yes, Jenny too—this afternoon when you were out with Alice.' Patrick looked unbearably smug. 'She's all for the idea—so is David, by the way. Naturally I consulted him first.'

'Why naturally?' said Carey indignantly. 'It's Jenny who'll be looking after Alice.'

'I knew Jenny would say yes without hesitation, so I thought it best to sound out David first. If he'd felt his wife wasn't up to it I would have had to think up something else. Actually, he was quite enthusiastic, especially when he heard Dilys had plans to feed him with that boned duck thing she did when he was here.'

'You, Patrick Savage, are adept at getting your own way!'

He smiled, unrepentant. 'In this instance, Carey, I feel my own way is most definitely what's best—for you as well as me.' His eyes met hers, their expression suddenly so tender her breath caught. 'I'm conscious that I've rushed you into all this, but it's the best time for me to get away, with the teleplay for *Privileged Class* finished, and the next book still mulling about in my brain. Even though this marriage of ours is a bit different from the usual kind I still think it's a great idea to go off together and spend a little while away from Llynglas and Alice and everything else, just getting to know each other better.'

Carey spread butter carefully on her water-biscuit. 'I suppose you're right. And that way I shan't have to worry about the baby, and you can forget all about television scripts and producers and agents and have a good rest.'

'Which, wife-to-be, is something you need far more than I do. You've looked peaky ever since Alice's chicken-pox. And you're too thin.'

'Armitages are always thin.'

'Perhaps you'll change once you're a Savage— like me!'

During the period between her decision to marry Patrick Savage and the actual date of the wedding, Carey found herself growing gradually more ac-customed to the idea. Apart from the family, no one had any idea about the coming nuptials except Dilys, who sat down in her chair by the table and had a good cry when she heard the news.

'I think it's lovely,' she sniffed. 'That dear little child will have a mother, and Mr Patrick will have a proper wife to make a home for him this time, not like before.' Dilys looked uncomfortable. 'Not that it's for me to talk, of course, but the other one was more interested in her career than looking after

Mr Patrick—and handsome though she was, she was years older than him, you know.'

Only Patrick wouldn't really have a proper wife, not in the accepted sense of the word, reflected Carey, and wondered, not for the first time, if she was doing the right thing. Patrick Savage, whatever he felt like now in the aftermath of Stephanie's death, might one day find his wounds healed and want a normal married relationship. But would she find that so impossible? thought Carey in sudden surprise. Was she so very, very sure, after all, that it was out of the question for her to think of him as a lover, in place of the one man in the world totally out of her reach? Perhaps now was the time to give up her pipe-dreams. Her future husband was an attractive, intelligent man. A man, moreover, who made it plain that he considered Carey to be an attractive, intelligent woman. And she liked it. And suffered pangs of guilt in consequence over her mental infidelity to a man who had probably, she assured herself, long since forgotten all about her.

Despite a period of panic in the small hours of the day itself, when the bride lay awake, tormented by doubts in her wisdom over marrying anyone at all, let alone Patrick Savage in particular, the wedding was a happy affair that went off smoothly from start to finish, from the brief church ceremony in Llanfach to the wedding reception prepared by Dilys and her cohorts from the village. The number of guests had been strictly limited, so that the dining-room in the tower had room to spare for David and Jenny Armitage, Mrs Savage, Charles

Collins, Patrick's agent and his eccentric, charming wife, Sadie, and Lewis and Gloria Morgan, the American owners of the beach house where Patrick had gone to ground after Stephanie's death.

Patrick was in tearing form the entire day, with no vestige of shadow on his jubilant face as he toasted his bride. Mrs Savage Senior had a tear in her eye as Patrick circulated among his guests with Alice in his arms, proudly insisting that the noises she cooed up at him sounded like 'Daddy'.

'I hope she didn't cry when she got back from her walk with Dilys and found me gone,' said Carey that evening, when, utterly exhausted after the travelling and excitements of the day, they were relaxing over a late supper in their room at the secluded Portuguese hotel finally chosen for their holiday.

'Even if she did, Alice won't cry for the whole two weeks we're away. So, Madam Wife, try to forget about my daughter for the time being and concentrate on keeping her father amused instead.' Patrick smiled across at her reassuringly. 'You looked utterly ravishing today, Carey. You do tonight, for that matter, but you knocked me for six in that hat as you came down the aisle.'

'I'm pleased to hear it—it was very expensive!' said Carey with feeling. 'Jenny bullied me into buying it because it went with the outfit. I've never paid so much money out on one item in my life.'

Patrick shook his head reprovingly. 'You don't have to worry about money any more.'

She grinned. 'I didn't before. I earn—earned—good money as a nanny, you know. It's just that frivolous hats were never a requirement then.'

The hat in question was large, made of grey silk with white, coin-sized dots, like the jacket which topped the plain grey silk skirt of her suit.

'I'll take you to Ascot next year so that you can wear it again!'

'It'll probably be out of fashion by then.'

'Then I'll buy you whatever *is* in fashion, and take you to Ladies' Day just the same—if you'd like that, of course.'

'Oh, I would,' Carey assured him, eyes sparkling. 'I've always wanted to go to a smart race meeting, with champagne and all the trimmings.'

'Then you shall.' Patrick took a bottle from its nest of ice in the bucket beside him, and filled their glasses before toasting Carey with the vintage champagne he'd ordered as appropriate for the occasion. 'To us, then, Mrs Savage. May we be happy together.'

'Amen,' said Carey, with a fervour which quite plainly met with her new husband's approval.

Their suite was the best the hotel had to offer, with adjoining rooms each with its own bathroom, a sitting-room and a balcony which looked out on a stretch of south-facing Atlantic coast where surf thundered far below and the scent of pines rose through the windows Carey had asked to be opened to the starlit night.

'Not the most lively place in the world,' commented Patrick. 'But it's comfortable, the food is good and the service impeccable and very friendly, did you notice? Just the place for you to unwind and get some colour back in your cheeks.'

'I think it's perfect,' said Carey, and stifled a yawn, smiling at him apologetically. 'It's been a long day. I didn't sleep much last night.'

'Alice wakeful?'

'No. I got the jitters in the small hours, in true bridal style.'

'Plagued by second thoughts?'

Carey's eyes were reflective as they rested on the tall, elegant man in the lightweight tweed jacket, his hair gleaming gold above a face less fine-boned and hollowed than at their first meeting, but still retaining some of its California tan.

'Well?' he prompted, his eyes intent. 'Did you want to back out at the last minute after all? You could have, you know.'

'I do know. I'll admit the thought did cross my mind, then I heard Alice murmur in her sleep, and realised I was just being silly.'

He shook his head, a wry twist to his mouth as he investigated the refrigerator hiding inside a heavy carved cabinet in one corner of the room. 'I'm glad my daughter changed your mind. How about a nightcap?'

'Thank you, I'm still very thirsty.' Carey sat down on the sofa near the window, looking out on the lights of the village in the distance. 'It's so peaceful here.'

'It's peaceful at Llynglas, too,' he reminded her. 'I thought you'd have fancied something more hectic for a change.'

'This place sounded so appealing,' she said, feeling oddly uneasy now they were alone together, with supper over and nothing left to do but go to bed. Patrick gave her a tall, ice-filled glass then mixed himself a drink. Carey downed half her own almost in one swallow, then realised too late that there was gin in the fruit juice. The spirit hit her with the kick of a mule, and she gasped, feeling giddy and disorientated, looking about her wildly for somewhere to deposit the drink.

Patrick took the glass from her hastily. 'Hey! You weren't supposed to knock it back like that, for Pete's sake.'

'I—thought it was fr-fruit juice,' she said with difficulty, opening her eyes wide to combat the whirling sensation in her brain. 'I had cham-champagne, too—and I can't drink, y'know...' She gave up, her eyes closing as she subsided in a huddle into the corner of the sofa. 'Sorry,' she muttered indistinctly.

'Hell,' said Patrick, staring down at her. 'Carey— Carey! Can you stand up?'

She nodded solemnly, then winced as her head spun like a top. With an almighty effort she struggled to sit up, then a jaw-splitting yawn vanquished her and she flopped back again.

Patrick gave a strangled laugh. 'Oh, dear, oh, dear. You, Carey Savage, are drunk.'

'Not!' she protested, snuggling her cheek against a cushion. 'Just tired.' She surrendered to the drowsiness conquering her, barely aware of being lifted in her new husband's arms as he carried her into her room and laid her on the bed.

'Carey!' said Patrick sharply.

'Mm.'

'Can you undress yourself?'

'Mm.'

'Oh, for heaven's sake,' he said, half laughing, half scolding. 'Come on, lend a hand, girl.'

Carey held up her arms obediently, but Patrick sighed.

'No, no. Turn over on your front so I can undo your zip.'

Carey tried hard to do as he'd said, but her co-ordination was hopeless. After one or two futile attempts she felt Patrick's hard hand flip her over like a rag doll, and she lay face down while he pulled down the zip and peeled her new pink linen dress away.

'There,' he said gruffly. 'That should do.' He tugged the covers away from beneath her, then drew them up over her, and went off with her dress to hang it up.

Carey watched him sleepily, only half aware of what was happening. She felt the bed depress as he put one knee on it to bend to kiss her cheek, and she smiled a little and turned to burrow into the pillow, leaving her husband to take himself quietly from the room.

When she woke it was light, and she had a raging thirst, a splitting headache and felt utterly appalled to find herself still attired in slip, bra, knickers and stockings, all of them brand-new and silk and pretty, but not what she'd have chosen to wear to bed. She groaned and staggered out of bed, making blindly for the bathroom. She stripped off her clothes and stood under the shower, washing her hair with the shampoo provided by the hotel, then wrapped herself in one of the hotel bathsheets and went back into the bedroom to find Patrick leaning in the doorway, attired only in dark red pyjama trousers, looking every bit as deathly as Carey felt.

'Good morning,' he said hoarsely. 'Are you all right?'

'No, I'm not,' she said bitterly, feeling too wretched to care that her hair was hanging in a wet tangle down her back, or that a towel was her only garment. 'I think I've got a hangover.'

'I *know* I've got a hangover,' he returned with equal bitterness.

'Why didn't you wake me up so I could undress?' she asked, eyes half closed against the pain as she searched for underwear in a drawer.

'I tried. You wouldn't.'

'I just can't cope with alcohol.'

'So I noticed. I don't think I can, either. Not as much as I used to, anyway.' He eyed her morosely. 'I don't suppose you'd have something for a headache?'

Carey nodded, then gasped, wishing she hadn't. 'I've got some fizzy pain-killers in my wash-bag.'

'Do they fizz fairly quietly?'

She managed a weak smile, then waved a hand towards her bathroom. 'The bag's in there.'

'Shall I fizz some for you, too?'

'Yes, please.'

While Patrick was out of sight Carey dived into her dressing-gown, wrapping herself in heavy cream satin as he returned with a foaming glass. Carey

seized on the glass eagerly and gulped down the
soluble aspirin, shuddering, then began very gin-
gerly to rub her hair dry.

Patrick, who was sporting a rather villainous
growth of dark blond beard, slumped down on the
edge of Carey's bed, eyeing her ruefully. 'All you
had, you know, was a couple of glasses of champagne and a shot of gin in about a pint of fruit
juice.'

'Which,' she retorted, 'is roughly a glass of
champagne and a shot of gin more than I can take.
I'm cursed with a weak head. I admit it. Normally
I respect it and act accordingly, but last
night——' she stopped, biting her lip, and bent her
head so that the long black hair streamed downwards to hide her face.

'But last night you felt awkward and shy and
suddenly unsure of the situation you'd landed
yourself in,' he said heavily. 'Were you afraid I'd
pounce on you and demand my conjugal rights after
all?'

Carey's face flushed scarlet behind the veil of
hair. 'No, of course not,' she snapped, feeling guilty
because he'd hit the nail square on the head.

'Carey, come out from under that hair and look
at me,' he commanded in a tone which demolished
any opposition.

She shook the damp hair back from her face and
with reluctance faced him across the width of the
bed. Patrick's bloodshot eyes held hers relentlessly.

'I've told you how I once took a woman against
my better judgement. I'll never make the mistake
again, believe me, Carey. You have my word.'

'Thank you,' she answered soberly. 'Not that I really thought you would, Patrick, honestly. After all, I'm not exactly the sort of female who inspires men to—to raging desire and so on. It's just that here, in what appears to be the bridal suite, and being our wedding night and all that, I suddenly felt a bit—apprehensive, I suppose.' Something suddenly struck her. She frowned at him. 'Which explains why *I* happen to have a hangover, but not why you've got one too.'

Patrick rose to his feet in one graceful movement and sauntered to the door, his back to her. 'It does, actually,' he said casually. 'Even I, my dear, was affected by the prevailing bridal atmosphere last night. The libido I once mentioned is not, I find, as defunct as I thought. But don't worry. My word's still good.'

Carey sat watching him dumbly as he turned to smile at her.

'By the way,' he informed her, 'you're wrong. This isn't the bridal suite. Bridal suites tend to have just the *one* bedroom—with just the one bed.' His eyes gleamed suddenly. 'You were wrong about the other thing, too.'

'What other thing?'

'The raging desire bit, Carey. In fact, you've got it hopelessly wrong about that. Take it from me, little wife, right this very moment you're alluring enough to inspire desire in any man, I assure you— including me.'

Carey stared aghast at the door as it closed behind her new husband's bare brown back, then rushed to the carved, antique wardrobe and snatched trousers and sweater from hangers, her hands trembling as she rummaged for fresh underwear in a drawer. She dressed at such speed her aching head was throbbing badly again by the time she began on her hair, and for once she cursed the length and thickness of it. It was still only half dry by the time Patrick put his head round the door.

'Come on, slowcoach,' he said cheerfully. 'I'm hungry.'

'Just give me a few minutes,' she muttered, avoiding his eye as she wielded a hair-drier.

'Leave it down,' he said promptly.

Carey hesitated, shot a look at Patrick, who smiled so encouragingly she gave in and brushed the half-damp mass away from her face, tying it at the back of her neck with a black chiffon scarf. 'Will that do?'

'Much better. You look a lot more human with your hair down for a change.'

'Maybe I'll even *feel* human if I have some coffee,' she muttered ruefully, and he laughed, taking her hand.

'Come on, some fresh orange juice—no gin this time—and some good strong coffee, plus some bacon and eggs, and you'll be fine.'

Carey blenched at the last bit. 'No food, please!'

'You must,' he insisted, as a discreet knock sounded on the outer door. 'And here it comes.'

Within minutes two waiters had laid the small table near the french windows opening on to the balcony, leaving a laden trolley near to hand, both young men smiling as they thanked Patrick for his lavish tip. He seated his new bride with a flourish behind the coffee-pot, the fragrance from it doing wonders for Carey's aching head almost at once, and to her surprise she found she was able to drink the promised orange juice and nibble at some chilled melon, and after a cup of coffee was even able to tackle the crisp grilled bacon Patrick insisted serving her.

'But no egg, please,' she said flatly. 'I have my limitations.'

Patrick grinned, and began on his own meal with gusto, looking a lot better himself now his hangover had begun to subside. 'I like the outfit,' he commented, eyeing Carey's white-trimmed black sweater with approval. 'Especially the nautical flags down the front.'

'Goes with the white trousers,' said Carey. 'Product of that mad shopping session with Jenny.'

'You should dress like that all the time.' He smiled at her. 'It suits you—and there's no need for all the prim nanny-gear any more.'

She flushed a little, and fussed with the coffee-pot, feeling suddenly shy at the look in his eyes, and Patrick smiled indulgently.

'Not used to breakfasting with a man, Carey!' His eyes narrowed suddenly. 'Which, of course, is complete supposition. I may have been laying my soul bare lately, but I still know very little about you, Mrs Savage.'

'Not much to tell,' she said lightly.

'You must have had men-friends in the past, Carey?'

'Of course. Several. But nothing serious.'

'Until this great love of your life who had the bad luck to marry someone else before he met you. Am I right?'

Carey spread butter on a piece of toast, gratified to see that her hand was steady. 'More or less,' she said, without looking at him. 'My life story in a nutshell.'

'Not quite,' he contradicted. 'There's a fair amount of it to go yet. But from now on, Carey, I think *I* merit the privilege of the central role in the story, instead of this chap you've been languishing over—whoever he may be.'

Carey lifted steady grey eyes to his. 'You *and* Alice,' she said pleasantly.

His mouth tightened as he pushed his coffee-cup towards her. 'Ah, yes. Alice. The *raison d'être* for this civilised marriage of ours.' He looked at her with an unsettling expression in his ink-dark eyes. 'I assume that without Alice you would never have even considered marrying me.'

Carey met the look serenely. 'Without Alice the question wouldn't have arisen, Patrick. Since I'm a nanny by profession, you and I would never have come across each other. I've never moved in literary circles.'

There was silence for a moment, then Patrick took the coffee-cup she passed him and nodded musingly. 'No. I suppose you're right. You soon will, though. Lewis Morgan's giving a party for us when we get back. His television company's putting out *Privileged Class* in the States next summer.'

'Wonderful! Congratulations, Patrick.' Carey raised her glass of orange juice and toasted him, smiling.

He grinned back. 'Got to keep the taxman happy, sweetheart.'

'Now you've finished the teleplay, what's on the agenda next?'

Nothing loath, Patrick plunged into a description of the next novel he had in mind, a topic which Carey found so absorbing they were still discussing it alongside the hotel pool later on in the morning, and which proved an effective antidote to any shyness Carey felt about displaying herself in a swimsuit which looked positively modest compared with some of the brief affairs worn by other women lounging beside the glittering blue pool.

'Not one of them has a shape as good as you,' said Patrick, and let himself down with a sigh of pleasure, face up to the sun.

Carey looked down at herself appraisingly, shot a discreet look at the other sunbathers and decided Patrick was right. She felt rather smug as she smoothed suntan lotion into her legs, and looked up to surprise a wicked gleam in Patrick's eyes as he watched her.

'First time I've had such an uninterrupted view,' he remarked. 'Your sunbathing sessions at the lake were very discreet affairs.'

'I should hope so,' Carey returned tartly. 'Nannies are required to be discreet——' She stopped dead in sudden pain, aware that her husband was watching her with eyes like a hawk.

'But you're not a nanny any more.' Patrick sat up and took the bottle for her. 'Lie down on your front and I'll oil your back.'

Carey did as he said, unwilling to argue since they were, if not exactly in earshot, at least within view of other people, and she lay flat, her face buried against the cushions, while Patrick smoothed the lotion over her back and legs with a light, impersonal touch which showed no disposition to linger, and after a moment or two he was back on his own sunbed, deep in discussion of his new book again.

'But, dear wife,' he warned that night over dinner, 'we shan't be lotus-eating like today all the time. Tomorrow we go out exploring.'

Carey was all for it. Since it was her first trip to Portugal she was perfectly happy to see as much of it as Patrick cared to show her. The hotel was situated near one of the south-facing beaches between Sesimbra and Portinho da Arrábida, where green hills fell sharply down to meet white sand and a translucent blue sea. On the journey by car from Lisbon late the previous evening it had been too dark to see much of the scenery, but Patrick had informed his tired, bemused bride that he was driving her along one of the older roads south towards Vila Nogueira de Azeitão, through orchards and pine-woods, where she would find the temperature wonderfully balmy, very much like the Mediterranean. Now Carey was eager to see more.

After a day of energetic sightseeing Carey found she felt far more relaxed later that night. They dined in the restaurant, and when it was time to go to their suite Patrick made them each a nightcap, himself a Scotch and Carey the plain tonic water she ordered with a grin, and after chatting about their itinerary for the next day they parted quite naturally with a kiss on Carey's cheek from Patrick and an admonition to be up and about not only early but a great deal brighter than on her first morning.

'You too,' said Carey pertly. 'Chauffeurs should avoid hangovers.'

The days assumed a pattern quite quickly. One day they went out in the car and explored as many local places of interest as Patrick deemed suitable for Carey without tiring her, the next they lay in the sun and read and slept and talked, and ate the delicious food for which the hotel was renowned.

There were hours at a time when Carey never gave a thought to Alice, nor to anyone else, she realised with a start of guilt one day. The area of Portugal known as the Arrábida became a world apart where Patrick laid claim to, and gained, her entire attention. Their first excursion together was to Azeitão, which Patrick informed his wife meant literally the 'little place of olives'. They drove to it past vineyards and olive-groves and woods to find a charming town which utterly captivated Carey and had her reaching immediately for her camera to take pictures of its disused palaces and alleyways and fountains, a pastime which Patrick had to drag her from, laughing, at last to eat lunch in a sixteenth-century inn full of the beautiful local blue tiles, the *azulejos* for which Portugal was famous. Flushed with excitement, Carey gazed in delight at the lake which formed part of the inn garden, utterly entranced by a cupola which appeared to float in the middle of the water, with swans gliding past to complete the picture.

'Just a little bit like Llynglas,' she said happily, 'only Llynglas doesn't have any swans, Patrick.'

'It's not going to, either!' he warned, grinning. 'Eat your *pudim de caramel* like a good girl, then this afternoon we'll inspect the local wine establishment, where I'm told they make the best dessert wine in the country.'

CHAPTER SEVEN

IT WAS, Carey decided early in the second week, by far the best holiday she'd ever had in her life. There had been trips to France and Spain with her parents and David as a child, and to Italy and Greece with friends on cheap package holidays when she'd been older, but the leisurely wanderings with Patrick in this region of Portugal eclipsed them all. For one thing he was extremely good company, no longer plagued these days by the melancholy of the moods which had still troubled him from time to time at Llynglas before their wedding. Stephanie was a ghost he seemed to have laid at last, Carey decided, and rejoiced for him that he had. Patrick Savage was a man she grew to like and appreciate more and more as time went by. And he had been right about the opportunity needed to get to know each other better. Carey found it remarkably easy to chatter away to him about her past experiences as a nanny, about her childhood, her schooldays, her parents; everything under the sun, in fact, except the one subject on which she still remained dumb. Patrick respected her privacy in this one dark area, to her gratitude, and never tried to encroach on it, though Carey was never left in doubt of his deep interest in the subject.

One sun-drenched, temperate day succeeded another as they explored. Carey captured scenes on film from every place they visited, bent on looking back with pleasure on their trips to some of the little icing-white towns of the flat, dry Alentejo, to the tombs and magnificent architecture of the two great abbeys of Alcobaça and Batalha, also to more secular places like Sesimbra and Setúbal, both busy fishing ports, one famous for its shellfish, the other for the Portuguese oyster.

Halfway through the second week Patrick called a halt to sightseeing, and decreed they spend the rest of the time either on the beach or beside the pool, doing nothing more strenuous than reading.

'Can't have you going back looking worn out,' he remarked, then stopped short, his eyes hidden behind his dark glasses.

Carey pretended to be absorbed in her novel, hoping her tan hid the quick colour in her cheeks. Most brides, she thought wryly, returned from honeymoon looking worn out for very different reasons from the activities she'd been engaged in with Patrick. The other guests in the hotel were friendly, but rarely intruded on the privacy of the newly-weds, though Carey often intercepted an appreciative feminine glance in Patrick's direction. This, she conceded, was only to be expected. After the days of sun and pine-scented, salt air, he looked more tanned and blond and eye-catching than ever, though with dark smudges beneath his eyes—the result, as Carey learned by accident one night, of sheer lack of sleep.

The balcony which linked the three rooms of their suite had french windows with glass, which afforded Carey a disturbing picture one night soon after their arrival, when she got up for a drink in the small hours. As she stood at the open window with her glass, she realised she could see Patrick's reflection quite plainly. He was seated in a chair near his window, fully dressed at two in the morning, with a glass in his hand, staring blindly out to sea. He had quite obviously not been to bed.

Carey said nothing next morning, nor at any other time after subsequent glimpses of him during the night, afraid that any comment on his nocturnal habits would not only be an intrusion, but might prompt him to give her the reason for them. And Carey shrank from learning why Patrick found it so difficult to sleep.

Towards the end of their stay they were invited to join a table with several other guests for the evening at a gala, a full-dress dinner-dance. Patrick displayed very little enthusiasm for the festivities when he strolled in to join Carey before dinner, looking very impressive in a white dinner-jacket which emphasised the darkness of his tan. Carey, her dressing-gown over her dress while she did her face and hair, was just putting the last touches to the knot she was twisting high on her head when Patrick knocked and strolled in to join her.

'I would have preferred to dine alone, as usual,' he said moodily, as he leaned at the open window to watch her.

Carey smiled consolingly. 'They seem like nice people, and it was kind of them to ask.'

'No doubt you welcome the idea with open arms,' he remarked, scowling.

Carey shrugged. 'Not particularly. We can stay up here, if you like, and have our dinner here. I don't mind.'

Patrick looked contrite. He pushed himself away from the glass door and came to join her at the mirror, smiling at her over her shoulder. 'I suppose I'm selfish, wanting my wife to myself. Particularly when she's spent rather more time than usual in creating such a ravishing effect. Of course we'll go down.' His eyes narrowed suddenly as they met the long grey ones in the mirror. 'I've never danced with you yet, have I? Do you dance well, Mrs Savage?'

'Brilliantly!' she assured him with a cheeky grin. She threaded pearl and gold hoops through her ears then slid the dressing-gown off her shoulders and turned to him. 'There. Will I do?'

Her dress was of oyster-coloured satin, a wickedly expensive little affair which Jenny had bullied her into buying. At the time its strapless simplicity had seemed a little stark, but now that Carey had a tan to rival Patrick's the dress gained a new dimension.

'Sensational,' breathed Patrick and took her by the hands, holding them far apart as his black eyes travelled over her, glittering with admiration—and something else which made Carey feel uneasy. There was a frankly proprietorial air about him as he escorted her down to dinner which made her wonder if a less spectacular dress might not have been a wiser choice, under their particular circumstances.

Later, on the small, darkened dance floor, Carey found that one thing she and her husband had very much in common was a sense of rhythm. They moved like one in time to the slow, late-night type of music provided by the small group hired from no less a place than Lisbon for this gala evening, and Patrick's hold became tighter and more possessive as the evening wore on. With punctilious good manners he danced with all three other ladies at the table, while Carey did the same with their partners, but from then on Patrick managed to make it clear in some indefinable way that he wished to dance only with his wife.

'And who could blame me?' he demanded later as they went up in the lift to their room, his dark eyes roving over her in a way which made Carey's heart lurch. Physically they remained inches apart, but Patrick's look sent shivers down her spine, tactile in its effect as it travelled from the crown of her black, glossy head to the tips of her toes and back again, and by the time the lift doors opened to let them out at their floor Carey felt as if every nerve were tuned to concert-pitch. She walked to their rooms ahead of Patrick, her cheeks blazing and her pulse erratic as the familiar long brown hand reached round her to unlock the door and let her in, the silence between them taut with tension for the first time since the night of their arrival.

Carey went straight through the sitting-room and into her bedroom, pausing at the door to bid Patrick goodnight in a stifled, breathless voice which brought him after her in two strides of his long legs, his hands gripping hers with a sudden intensity which sent her heart flying to her throat as she stared up into his face.

'Patrick——' she began, then gasped as he gave a sudden groan and pulled her against him, his cheek on her hair as he held her face against the thudding of his heart.

'I've tried—lord, how I've tried! But I can't keep to it. I want you, Carey,' he said in a voice so deep and hoarse she hardly recognised it, but his meaning was plain enough, since he suited action to words by picking her up and carrying her towards the bed.

'No, Patrick,' she panted, struggling in his arms, 'you gave your word!'

He laid her down on the bed, keeping her captive with one hand either side of her as he sat leaning over her, his face urgent. 'I know I did, but I never dreamed that I would ever want anyone again like this. I swear I never *have* wanted anyone so much. But I want you so badly, Carey, I've hardly slept since we arrived here, except for the odd doze by the pool. Do you realise what a superhuman effort I've been making to let you go every night with just a chaste kiss on the cheek, little wife? Do you know how many hours I spend in a chair in my room staring out over the sea while the lights in the village go out and leave me with only the stars for company?'

Carey nodded, trembling, unable to tear her eyes away from the flame in his. 'Yes. I do know. I—I've seen you.'

'*How?*'

She explained, swallowing drily. 'I should never have married you,' she finished dully. 'It was a mistake. You're a man, after all, and far too attractive to——'

Patrick gave a choked sound and caught her in his arms, his mouth smothering anything else she might have said, and Carey resisted valiantly, but his arms kept her still and his mouth, fierce at first, softened and began to woo hers into response. Carey trembled, rigid in his embrace, but after a while her resistance lessened. Unknown to herself, the days of sun and companionship had wrought a more powerful transformation in her than she would have believed possible. And tonight, moving together in sinuous harmony on the dance floor, there had been a response to her husband in her blood, no matter how hard she'd tried to ignore it. When Patrick had taken her away from the others everyone had quite plainly assumed he couldn't wait to take her to bed. And they were right, she realised in sudden panic, and pushed hard, and Patrick jumped away from her and leapt from the bed, tearing his collar open as he fled from the room.

Carey lay where he'd left her, breathless and shaken and unexpectedly tearful. What, she asked herself, was the matter with her? If she was honest she'd admit that Patrick Savage was a very attractive man, not only physically but in every other possible way. And the rest of her life was a long, long time to spend alone, lying in the bed she'd been determined to make for herself. The man she would have chosen to share a bed with was, at this very moment, beyond all doubt, sharing his with someone else. While she was here in Portugal, with a moon shining above, the surf pounding below— and, most important of all, it was her honeymoon. And at last she forced herself to come face to face

with the truth. Patrick's touch was not, nor ever
had been, in the least abhorrent. Far from it.

Slowly she slid off the bed and went over to the
dressing-table, grimacing at the mascara stains
below her eyes, at the hair tumbling down from its
elaborate knot. Swiftly Carey repaired the damage
and took down her hair, brushing it vigorously
while she nerved herself up to do the last thing in
the world she had believed herself capable of doing.
Yet one thing was clear. She'd spent far too long
fretting herself to fiddle strings over a man who
was never, ever going to be hers. In which case it
seemed hardly a sin to give herself to a man whom
she not only liked and respected, but who was now
her lawful wedded husband and entitled to everything she had to give.

But how, she thought in desperation, was she to
let Patrick know she'd changed her mind? Carey
stared at herself in the mirror, examining her reflection objectively, trying to see herself with her
husband's eyes. Her own glittered feverishly against
the glowing tan of her face, her cheek-bones flushed
with bright colour. The overall impression, thought
Carey, pulse racing, was so much that of a blushing
bride it really seemed a pity not to make the picture
complete in every way. She stood for a moment
longer, undecided, then crossed to the black, carved
chest to take out a garment she had not yet been
able to bring herself to wear. It had seemed a bit
silly to spend a vast sum on a nightdress under the
circumstances, but with Jenny for company on the
shopping trip it had been quite impossible to refuse
to buy at least one frivolous trifle.

Carey laid the handful of ivory silk and lace on the bed, then put her hands behind her back to undo her zip. She tugged, but the zipper moved only half an inch before it stuck, and Carey pulled on it impatiently. Then she paused, eyes narrowing. She would ask for help—much better than presenting herself like a sacrificial lamb all done up in her bridal finery. Before she could think better of it she went through into the sitting-room, tapped on Patrick's bedroom door and went in. He was sitting in his usual place by the window, staring out to sea, a half-empty glass of Scotch in his hand, and so sunk in gloom he was unaware of her presence until her light touch on his shoulder had him on his feet, staring at her in astonishment.

'Carey! Something wrong?'

'My zip's stuck,' she said baldly, trying to smile. 'Could you give me a hand?' She turned to present her back to him and heard Patrick's sharp intake of breath, then she clenched her teeth at the brush of his fingers on her bare skin as he tried to move the zip.

'It's caught on the fabric,' he said in a constricted voice. 'Perhaps if I sit down I can see better.'

Carey kept her head averted as she heard him turn the chair round, then Patrick's hands, purposely light at her waist as he guided her back against his knees. She kept her head bowed and her jaw clenched together to stop her teeth from chattering as she felt his hands unsteady against her as he applied himself to a task which began to appear hopeless.

'I can't sleep in the dress,' said Carey breath-lessly. 'You'll just have to tear it a bit if necessary.'

'Pity to do that.' Patrick gave a sudden yank which proved too much for the delicate slipper-satin. The dress came apart in his hands, Carey was jerked back against his knees, which parted invol-untarily, and she sat down suddenly on his lap. Patrick groaned like a man in pain, his hands sliding round her ribs to cup her breasts as the dress fell away. His mouth was hot against the nape of her neck as her hair hung down to expose it, and be-neath her thighs Carey felt a hard stirring which took her breath away, and suddenly she realised there was no need for her to say anything at all. Trembling a little, she turned in his arms and held up her face, and he drew her slowly upwards against his chest, kissing her with such tenderness that her mouth opened to him without hesitation and his arms crushed her to him convulsively. At her in-voluntary gasp they slackened and Patrick pushed her away a little to gaze down into her face in fierce question.

'Carey?' His eyes bored into hers, fathomless as pools of jet beneath the bright, tousled hair. 'Go now if you're going.'

'I'm staying,' she said gruffly, and buried her face against him.

'Are you sure?' he said into her hair. 'Not just for now, but always, remember. If I take you, I keep you.'

But even as he spoke he was smoothing and ca-ressing her skin with his long, clever fingers, touching off sparks of response as his hand moved over her spine and her collar-bone, then down to her breasts, and she gasped and stiffened in his arms as his fingers found the erect, quivering tips, bare now as her dress fell to her waist.

'Please——' she said indistinctly, and Patrick bent his bright head and kissed her hard until she was dizzy and breathless, helpless to resist when he moved his attention to her throat, lingering where a pulse throbbed madly at his touch, and Carey thrust herself involuntarily against him as he moved his mouth lower to replace his fingers with his lips at her breast. Carey felt as though her heart were being drawn out of her as he closed his teeth delicately on a nipple and caressed it lovingly with his tongue, and she could stand no more.

'Patrick!' she implored raggedly, and with one convulsive movement he stood up with her in his arms and laid her down on the bed. Very gently, as if savouring every move, he undressed her, then gazed at her in silence for a moment, his face colourless beneath the tan. Her eyes gleamed crystal-clear as she reached up her arms to him, and in seconds he'd thrown off his clothes and joined her on the bed, taking her in his arms with a sigh of pleasure which disarmed her utterly and completely.

Carey's limited experience of the opposite sex had not prepared her for someone like Patrick Savage. He maintained an iron control over his own urgency as he began on a slow, tantalising exploration of her body, finding those places most responsive to his touch and lingering there to tease and torment, sometimes with his lips, sometimes with delicate, probing fingers until she writhed against the pillows, her hair a wild tangle as her head threshed to and fro.

'I never thought it would be like this,' she panted at one stage, as Patrick paused to hold her close in an embrace which for a few much-needed moments was all tenderness and protection, but which proved to be merely the eye of the storm of sensual pleasure which followed. Carey was so drunk and dazed with love by the time he finally allowed himself the ultimate, shuddering pleasure of their union that she had no thought to spare for surprise at her body's all-out surrender to the wild, thudding rhythm which very quickly brought them both to an intensity of fulfilment almost painful in its exquisite abandon.

Afterwards there was no respectable lull while Carey came to earth. Patrick sat up, raking the hair away from his glistening forehead as his eyes met hers in burning question.

'Well?' he demanded.

Carey lay supine, finding it almost an effort to blink. 'Yes.'

'What do you mean, "yes"?' he demanded roughly, propping a hand either side of her.

'You asked if I was well. I am.' Carey smiled drowsily.

'No regrets?'

'Did it look like it?' she said crossly, and Patrick's sudden joyous grin stripped ten years from his face.

'No,' he admitted. 'Unless you're the most accomplished actress in the world, Mrs Savage, I think I may safely assume that what we just experienced together was at least half as miraculous for you as it was for me.'

'Oh, yes,' she agreed gravely. 'At least half!'

Whereupon Patrick fell to kissing her again, and, Carey dimly suspected, would quite possibly have gone on to do a great deal more than kiss her if she had given him the slightest bit of encouragement. But with a forbearance she felt was admirable Patrick picked her up and carried her into her own room to sleep.

'Stay with me,' she said softly as he laid her down, and smiled up at him in artless invitation, and Patrick turned back the covers and slid in beside her, holding her close in his arms.

'I thought you might prefer to sleep alone.'

Carey shook her head and wriggled closer. 'Now we've begun to be married properly, so to speak, we might as well go the whole hog.'

'Not the most graceful way in the world of phrasing it, Mrs Savage, but I'm in complete agreement with the sentiments.' He sighed deeply as his long body relaxed against hers.

'What's the matter?' murmured Carey.

'I was thinking it's a pity we have to go home in a couple of days. I would have liked to stay lotus-eating with you here a lot longer—especially...'

'Especially under the circumstances,' said Carey matter-of-factly, and felt her husband shake with laughter against her.

'Exactly,' he agreed, kissing her. 'I find these particular ''circumstances'' so ravishing all I want in this world is to stay here with you in this bed and sleep until it's time to drive back to the airport.'

'Not surprising, really, if you haven't been sleeping well since we got here.' Carey turned in his arms and kissed his cheek. 'I hope you sleep tonight.'

'No doubt about that. What better cure for insomnia could a man ask for?'

Carey giggled, then frowned in the darkness. 'Pity about my nightgown, though.'

'What nightgown?' he demanded, mystified.

'It's probably on the floor somewhere by now. I'd laid it out all ready to get into and come and seduce you, Patrick. But my zip stuck and ruined the whole thing.' She felt him stiffen beside her, then he reached out a hand to turn on the light beside the bed.

'Is that true?' he asked, his eyes narrowed to glittering black slits.

Carey nodded. She leaned out of the bed and gathered up the silk and lace confection lying on the floor beside it. 'This,' she informed him, 'is the nightie in question. Pretty, isn't it?'

'You mean you were going to come to me anyway, zip or no zip?' he asked carefully.

Carey's eyes fell before the look in his as she nodded. 'Will you put out the light now?'

Patrick obeyed, then slid back down in the bed and took her in his arms again. 'Carey,' he said casually.

'Mm?'

'Will you do something for me?'

'Yes.'

'Tomorrow night will you wear the nightgown for me, just so I can see how you planned to seduce me—not, heaven knows, that it was the least bit necessary!'

'All right. I will. Because tonight, after—after you left me alone, I had a serious think, you see, Patrick, and I came to the conclusion it was time to forget the past for both of us. Besides,' she added thoughtfully, 'if you must go back looking so haggard, at least let it be for the right reason!'

Patrick gave a roar of laughter which Carey shushed frantically, sure that he would wake the other guests.

'All right, all right,' he said unsteadily. 'But if you want to keep me quiet there's a simple way to do it.'

'Oh?'

'Just kiss me.'

'Ah! And if I do will you promise to be quiet?'

He chuckled deep in his throat. 'Try it and find out.'

But what Carey did find out was that one kiss was more than enough to set them both on fire for each other again, all thought of sleep forgotten as the astonishing response her husband roused in her proved as all-consuming as before, Patrick even more exultant now that he realised his wife had come to him of her own accord to share in an experience neither of them had ever envisaged when they had first embarked on their civilised, platonic marriage.

CHAPTER EIGHT

ON A cold December evening, almost two months after the return from Portugal, Carey emerged from her new house in one of the prettiest streets in Westminster to duck into the taxi waiting to take her to the smart riverside apartment, where Charles and Sadie Collins were holding what the latter referred to as a frightfully posh knees-up for Charlie's pet clients.

Carey felt a little tense as the car travelled in the direction of fashionable Docklands, mainly because she had to make an entry alone. Patrick was meeting her at the party later, coming straight from a radio interview. She smiled to herself a little ruefully. Even now, several weeks into her marriage, she still had problems in coming to terms with the fact that her handsome, clever husband was so successful. Ever since their return from Portugal he'd rushed her along on a wave of enthusiasm which had left her gasping at times. Winter in Llynglas was no place for the civilised, according to Patrick, and in next to no time the main house had been under covers, Dilys left as caretaker, and Patrick had whisked Carey and Alice off to stay with his mother for a week or two while he found them a house in London.

Mrs Savage had been delighted with the arrangement, though doubtful that Patrick would

succeed in installing his little family in a new home
before Christmas. She had been wrong. Her son,
invincible in his belief that his luck had changed
with marrying Carey, had found a house, *circa*
1870, complete with the garden at the back his wife
considered essential for their daughter's welfare.
The house had a fanlighted front door and sash
windows, and an iron rail either side of steps leading
down into a street which retained some of its
Victorian lamp-posts. From the outside, according
to Patrick, the Savages' new home looked as though
Sherlock Holmes ought to be in residence on the
upper floor.

Even now, thought Carey, it was hard to believe
that they were actually living there already, all the
red tape and conveyancing cut short to an unbelievable degree to make it possible for them to
move in only two short weeks previously. Admittedly they were almost camping out at the moment,
with only a modicum of furniture, some of which
had been borrowed from Llynglas, the rest bought
wherever they found something not only to their
taste but available for immediate delivery. All
Patrick's previous possessions had been sold at
auction. Apart from Alice, he wanted no reminders
of his marriage to Stephanie.

Carey felt a warm glow as she remembered the
welcome the baby had given them when they'd col-
lected her from Jenny and David. Alice's plump
little face had lit up like a beacon at the sight of
them, and she'd hurled herself into Carey's outstretched arms, crying 'Mum-mum-mum' in no uncertain manner, then had topped her performance

by turning to Patrick, with a smug look so like the one he could assume on occasion that Carey had crowed with laughter, as the gilt-haired charmer had beamed at her father and uttered 'Dad-dee' with such deliberate coquetry he had been completely bowled over.

The same little charmer had made Carey late this evening, because, as always with the young, she had sensed that something was up and had taken more settling down than usual. At least, Carey thought with satisfaction, she need have no qualms about Alice's safety in the hands of Catriona Mackay, the dependable young Scots girl she'd taken on to help with the child. Catriona was not exactly a nanny— more an au pair, if such a Gallic description could be applied to someone so Scottish. The calm, sandy-haired girl had been wonderful with Alice from the start, and perfectly happy to help out in any way Carey required, particularly with the sessions of baby-sitting it was obvious were to be necessary now the Savages had taken up residence in the capital.

After she'd paid off the taxi-driver outside the elegant new apartment block, Carey went up in the lift feeling apprehensive. Not that this was the first party she'd been to. The Morgans' reception to celebrate Patrick's mini-series had been a very splendid affair. At the time her tan had still been intact and Patrick had insisted on the white satin dress, complete with new zip, since, he told her with a glint in his eyes, not only did she look like a bride in it, but he had an enormous fondness for that particular dress. Tonight she looked very different, in ankle-length gold Paisley brocade; a narrow tube of a dress with high neck and long sleeves, and over it she wore the dramatic black velvet cloak Patrick had insisted buying for her at the same time.

'My word, you do look stunning,' said Sadie Collins, who was wearing layers of beaded crimson chiffon and a black feather boa, and Carey relaxed, deciding her own outfit was positively restrained in comparison. She apologised for her lateness as her hostess took her by the hand and sailed through open double doors into a huge raftered room lined with windows which looked straight down on to the Thames, and at first glance seemed to be populated by half of London.

The noise was terrific, but as Sadie hove into view with her velvet-clad companion in tow there was a lull in the conversation and all heads seemed to turn in their direction. Carey felt a moment of panic, then smiled, radiant with relief, as Patrick cut his way mercilessly through the throng and kissed her, oblivious of amused, watching eyes.

'Where the hell have you been?' he demanded, as he undid the gilt clasp beneath her chin.

'Alice played up,' said Carey, smiling happily at her husband, who, though dressed like all the other men in formal black dinner-jacket, to her eyes was easily the best-looking man in the room.

'Give me that cloak, darling,' said Sadie Collins, beaming at them fondly. 'Now I know you're still newly-weds, you two, but do stop canoodling and *mingle*. Charlie will ply you with drink, Carey, and later there are a few oddments to eat, when the rest of the guests arrive.'

'I'm not the last, then,' said Carey, flushing a little as Patrick gave her a hotly possessive look once Sadie had fluttered off.

'Apparently not,' he said absently, and breathed in deeply. 'How does that dress manage to cover you practically from top to toe, and yet look sexy as hell?'

'You chose it!'

'I must have been crackers. If I'd been at home when you were dressing I'd never have let you out in it.'

'Are you serious?' she demanded, alarmed, looking down at herself.

'No, my angel—well, not entirely,' Patrick amended, then put an arm round her waist to guide her through the crowd to Charles Collins, who was dispensing drinks from an array of bottles arranged on a slab of marble supported by crouching gilt lions.

'Carey!' he said, with pleasure. 'Have some champagne.'

'Only half a glass, Charlie,' said Patrick, and grinned at Carey. 'After that she's on ginger ale.'

'I suppose one of you has to keep sober,' said their host gaily, then began introducing Carey to so many people that her head reeled as she tried to match names to faces, and found one or two of them well-known to her from the dust-covers of novels she'd read. One lady in particular, celebrated for her complex crime novels, proved utterly fascinating, and Patrick had to drag his wife away at last to sample some of Sadie's 'oddments', which proved to be one of the most delicious suppers Carey had ever tasted. She perched with Patrick on a window-seat with a knot of television people for company, and found she was enjoying herself enormously as she voiced her opinion on the casting of Patrick's forthcoming mini-series. He sat as close to her as he could get, with a 'hands-off' look about him no one could fail to misinterpret, and Carey found she rather liked it, secretly laughing at herself because she felt so flattered.

'Penny for your thoughts,' said Patrick, his lips warm against her ear, and Carey turned to him with a smile.

'I was just thinking how lucky I am.'

Light leapt in the darkness of his eyes as they looked at each other, isolated for a moment from the noise and heat and laughter of the room. Patrick shook his fair head, slowly, his wide mouth curving in the smile he kept for her alone. 'I'm the lucky one, Carey.'

Sadie interrupted them, clucking her disapproval. 'I *said* no canoodling, darlings. Now come and meet some latecomers. You're the flavour of the month these days, Patrick, me boy. We've got some visitors from over the pond who want to meet the author of *Privileged Class*, so come and make like a celebrity, and bring Carey with you—unless you fancy leaving her to the mercy of this lot.' She waved a dismissive hand at the chorus of hoots and cat-calls which greeted this, and shepherded Patrick and Carey into the other room like a border collie rounding up her flock.

Sadie made for a group of people standing just inside the door: two tall men, and two exquisitely groomed women, one svelte and dark, the other one blonde with that milk-fed, peaches-and-cream bloom found in so many American beauties.

At the sight of them Carey felt a sickening thump in her chest. Her heart faltered, then resumed a heavy, thudding beat as the blonde woman gave a cry of delight and held out her hands.

'Carey Armitage! How wonderful to *see* you! Fancy meeting you here.' She turned to her husband. 'Look, Brad, it's Carey.'

Brad Stephenson was a tall, rangy man with the craggy good looks of a young Abraham Lincoln, and for a fleeting moment, as he turned towards Carey, his face could well have been carved of the same stone as the presidential faces on Mount Rushmore.

'To be accurate,' said Patrick smoothly, 'it's Carey Savage now.'

Ellen Stephenson's blue eyes opened saucer-wide. '*You're* Patrick Savage, and you've married our Carey?'

'*My* Carey now, actually.'

'Why, hello,' said Carey, finding her voice at last. 'What a surprise. Are you here on holiday?' Her nails bit into her palms in an effort to keep calm as she managed to pin a smile on her face as she turned to Patrick. 'I used to work for Mr and Mrs Stephenson. I looked after their children.'

Patrick held out his hand to the other man. 'How do you do?' he said with austere formality.

Brad Stephenson took the long, slim hand and shook it perfunctorily. 'Hi. Nice to meet you.' He turned stunned eyes back in Carey's direction. 'You look—great, Carey.'

'Thank you.' Carey gave him a bright, polite smile. 'How are Dean and Abby? Are they with you?'

'Sure. We're at the Waldorf. Staying here over Christmas, then we go to Hanover.'

'Can you come and see them?' asked Ellen Stephenson eagerly. 'They'd just love to have you visit, Carey, and show you their new little brother Brad. I can't wait to tell them we met you.'

Patrick looked down at Carey with a gleaming, tigerish smile. 'Now we've got Catriona to keep an eye on the baby we'd be glad to.' He shot a quick look at Brad, who looked as though someone had just punched him in the stomach. 'Or perhaps you'd like to bring your family to visit *us*? We've only just moved into our present home, so we're rather roughing it at the moment, but you're welcome to come and see where Carey lives these days.' His drawl was very pronounced, Carey realised with a sinking heart, recognising the danger sign of old.

'That would be wonderful,' said Ellen Stephenson with enthusiasm. 'We'd just love to visit your home, Mr Savage—only now we know you're married to our darling Carey, can we call you Patrick?'

'Certainly,' he said affably, then turned to Carey. 'I think Charles wants us, sweetheart.' He turned a dazzling white smile on both Stephensons, who suddenly realised they'd neglected to introduce their

friends from the American Embassy, the apologetic flurry of introductions a godsend in easing
the tension only Ellen Stephenson seemed unaware
of as Patrick detached his wife at last and took her
away to the far side of the room, where Charlie
Collins was making signals that their presence was
required.

Carey moved through the next few minutes like
an automaton. She smiled, even laughed when it
seemed appropriate, her hand in the crook of
Patrick's arm as she made the right responses to
the right people. Just as if, she thought dazedly,
I'd been programmed to behave like the perfect celebrity's wife. Quite a clever trick for someone in
shock. How intolerably small the world was, after
all, and what a place to have it proved, here in the
stronghold of literati which was Patrick's particular milieu. And the crowning, unbearable touch
was the knowledge that a certain pair of deep-set
blue eyes were trained on her back the entire time,
willing her to turn round.

Patrick glanced down at her after a time. 'You
look pale, Carey.'

'I'm fine. Just a bit tired.' She looked up at him
in entreaty. 'Could we go home soon, please?'

'Right now if you want,' he said tersely. 'Go and
find your cloak. I'll ring for a taxi.'

Carey pushed her way through the crowded room
to the corridor which led to the bedrooms. She
closed the door of Sadie's guest room behind her
and sank down on the edge of the bed for a
moment, limp with reaction. She buried her head
in her hands, then took in several deep, calming

breaths and took her velvet cloak from the chair
where Sadie had draped it. She put the hood up
over her hair, fastened the clasp beneath her chin,
then braced herself to leave the small, quiet haven
of the bedroom to rejoin the rest of the world. She
bent to inspect her face in the dressing-table mirror,
then froze as she saw the door open quietly behind
her. Very slowly, like someone in a nightmare, she
turned to face Brad Stephenson as he closed the
door behind him, barring her escape.

'I saw you slip away,' he said in the voice she
remembered so well, with its flat Boston vowels and
the note of assurance which came from a lifetime
of privilege and Brad Stephenson's confidence in
his own particular place in the scheme of things.

'I came to get my cloak,' said Carey distantly.
'You shouldn't be here.'

'Do you think I don't know that?' He put out
his hands suddenly and captured hers. 'I must see
you, Carey,' he said urgently.

'That's out of the question,' she retorted. 'Please
let me go.'

'*No!*' He took her by the shoulders and shook
her slightly, faint beads of perspiration dewing his
upper lip.

'You know perfectly well it's not possible,' she
said emphatically, and brushed past him, almost
running from the room to cannon straight into
Patrick at the end of the hall.

'Ready?' he said, his eyes icy as he stared past
her at Brad Stephenson, who stood like a statue,
watching them.

Carey nodded blindly.

'Right, then, let's go. The taxi's arrived. I've said your goodbyes.'

'Thank you,' she whispered as Patrick led her to the lift and stood beside her in silence all the way down to the lobby.

The killing silence continued as he handed her into the taxi, then took his own place beside her, only inches away from her on the seat, yet as remote from her as though he'd left her to travel home alone. When they arrived at the house Patrick paid off the driver, gave him a large tip, wished him Merry Christmas, then followed Carey into the house, where she went straight up to check on Alice and send Catriona off to her own little apartment in the basement.

Afterwards Carey stood irresolute before the mirror in the room she shared with Patrick, her eyes on the vast bed which had been Patrick's first purchase for their new home. Should she go back downstairs, or stay here like a coward and get ready for bed, pretending nothing was wrong? There was no real choice, of course, she thought drearily. The music, dissonant though it was bound to be, just had to be faced. She hung the cloak away then squared her shoulders and went downstairs to the sitting-room, where Patrick was standing in front of the fireplace, glass in hand, waiting for her. Her heart sank as she met eyes which burned like coals in his dangerously calm face.

'Would you like a drink?' he asked courteously.

'Yes. For once I would. Unfortunately I've already had my quota of alcohol for tonight.' Carey gave him a forlorn little smile. 'Sober seems hardly the word for how I feel, but that's how I'd better stay.'

'Won't you sit down?' said Patrick, so glacially polite that Carey shivered as she sat on the velvet sofa they had chosen together only a few days before, sorry already that she'd refused the drink. Alcoholic oblivion seemed a very seductive alternative to the forthcoming interview.

'Are you cold?' he asked.

'Not really.' How could she possibly describe this terrible chill she felt inside, as though her very soul were icing over?

'What were you doing in Sadie's bedroom with your American friend?' Patrick asked conversationally.

The blood rushed to Carey's face then drained away again, leaving her deathly pale. 'I went to get my cloak. He came after me. We were only there for a moment.'

'For a diplomat he's a trifle impetuous, wouldn't you say, rushing into a bedroom after another man's wife in the middle of a party?' Patrick strolled across the room to refill his glass, then turned, smiling the white, meaningless smile she detested. 'Let's hope Washington never posts him to Moscow.'

Carey's hands twisted together in her lap. 'It won't happen again, I promise.'

'*What* won't happen again?' He stalked across the room like a prowling panther, and stood over her, staring down into her face, apparently unmoved by the misery on it. 'Did anything happen before, Carey? While you worked for your Mr

Stephenson, I mean? Did he indulge in a spot of droit de seigneur, possibly? Where, Carey? In his bed when his wife was out having her hair done? Or possibly you had some secluded little attic under his diplomatic roof where he could creep at night when the fair Ellen had a headache.'

'Don't!' she cried in anguish, pushing him aside as she jumped to her feet. She stood in front of the fireplace, facing him squarely. 'It was nothing like that.'

'*Tell* me how it was, Carey,' he commanded, breathing faster. 'I want to know. I have the right to know, don't you think? You are, after all, my wife.'

'Whom you married,' said Carey, eyes blazing suddenly, 'in the knowledge that she cared for someone else. I have not, in *any* way, deceived you about that. The only thing I kept from you was the identity of the man.'

'Who else knows about him?'

'No one.'

'Jenny? David?'

'No. It just so happened Jenny needed me at the time Brad—the Stephensons—were returning to Washington. It was assumed I gave up my job to look after Paul. Which, heaven knows, I did.' Carey thrust a hand through her hair in a sudden, wild gesture, dislodging some of the gold pins which held it up. 'If I hadn't gone to David in Cardiff I'd have found another job somewhere, believe me. It was no longer possible to—to remain where I was.'

Patrick sat down abruptly, as though his legs had given out. He stretched them out in front of him, staring at the carpet. '*Did* you sleep with him, Carey?'

She closed her eyes for a moment, then opened them again. 'Will you believe me if I say no?'

'I *want* to believe you,' he said passionately. 'Tell me what happened. Now. Then I swear I'll never utter a word on the subject again.'

Carey sat down beside him on the sofa, feeling unutterably weary as she tried to be as objective as possible in her account of her early days in the busy Stephenson household. From the first, Ellen Stephenson had taken to the calm new English nanny and had insisted on first names, treating Carey like one of the family. For a while Brad Stephenson had hardly seemed to notice that Carey had been around. But after she had been persuaded to eat dinner with them now and again, or go with the family on trips to the country and the 'shore', as Ellen had described it, his attitude towards Carey had gradually begun to change. In a hundred small ways he had let her know he had been attracted to her, and Carey, utterly dazzled by him, had fallen hopelessly in love without even so much as a kiss exchanged.

'Things must have taken a different turn at some stage,' said Patrick grimly.

'They did.'

'What happened?'

The Stephensons had taken the children home to Boston to stay with their grandparents one Christmas, which Carey had spent in Cardiff with David and Jenny. When she'd returned to London, as arranged, only Brad had been in residence at the house. Abby had developed a cold just before leaving, making Ellen decide to remain behind with the children for another week while her husband had flown back to London on his own.

'You were alone in the house with him?'

Carey shook her head. 'There was a cook, but she only came in daily, also there was a cleaning firm who came in to see to the house two or three times a week. We were alone only at night.'

'Quite the best time, wouldn't you say?' The distaste in his voice cut her to ribbons.

'It wasn't *like* that, Patrick! It just so happened that he was exceptionally busy at the time and came home late most evenings, long after the cook had gone. She used to leave various things in readiness, and I—I would make supper for him when he came home. He insisted I share it with him.' Carey's eyes met Patrick's unhappily. 'We—we talked a lot, enjoyed each other's company. We found we had quite a lot in common.'

'When did he take you to bed?' said Patrick swiftly, his eyes boring into hers.

Carey glared at him in sudden temper. 'He never, ever took me to bed!'

'Are you telling me the man never touched you?' Patrick gave a scornful laugh. 'I saw for myself tonight, remember! His gorgeous blonde wife apparently never even noticed, but to me, my darling wife, it was blindingly obvious the guy was knocked for six at the sight of you.'

'It was just surprise at meeting so unexpectedly,' said Carey desperately, but Patrick hooted in derision.

'His wife was surprised, too, but she didn't come chasing into a bedroom after you!'

'All right,' said Carey militantly, tired of the defensive. 'In words of one syllable, Patrick Savage, since you won't rest without a blow-by-blow account of what actually did or didn't happen, the very night before Ellen was due back Brad held the door of the dining-room open for me after supper and I smiled up at him as I said goodnight and he—he kissed me, and told me he'd been in love with me for months.'

There was silence in the room for some time after that, broken only by the crackle of a log as the fire died to ashes.

'Go on,' said Patrick at last, as though the words were torn out of him.

Carey gave a forlorn little shrug. 'I let him go on kissing me. I'd been kissed before, of course, but I suppose it was the things he said which made me fall apart the way I did. I'm not proud of it. I knew better than anyone that there was nothing for me in caring for Brad Stephenson in any way at all. But it made no difference. He—he very much wanted to be my lover. But that was impossible. Not that I didn't want him—I must be honest about that—but because of Ellen and the children. I lay awake in utter misery all that night, knowing I had no choice but to leave immediately. Fate, in a way, was kind. First thing next morning I had a cry for help from David because Jenny had hurt her back. So when Ellen arrived in the afternoon with Dean and Abby I was packed and ready to go, my reason tailor-made.' She turned to look Patrick in the eye. 'I never saw Brad Stephenson again, until tonight.'

Patrick stared back with blank, sleepwalker's eyes. 'Did he ever imply that there might be some kind of future for you—together, I mean?'

Carey gave him a bitter little smile. 'Oh, no. Out of the question. Bradley Stephenson the Third comes from a long line of gold-carat Back Bay Bostonians. Ellen too. But the most important thing they have in common is their religion. They're Catholic.'

'No luck for a Protestant English nanny of more charm than family tree, then,' said Patrick cruelly. 'Maybe *that's* what made you leave.'

'No. It wasn't.' Carey's mouth twisted. 'I've been brought up quite well, hard though you may find it to believe. Lovesick I might have been, but once Brad kissed me I knew I had no choice but to leave.'

'So you left as a matter of principle.'

'Yes. Even without Jenny's problem I would have gone just the same. But as it happened there was something else too, by way of a final straw.' Carey's chin lifted. 'But that's one thing I can't bring myself to talk about—not even to you.'

Patrick tossed back the rest of his whisky. 'Is it so utterly sacrosanct, then?'

'Not in the least. Just humiliating.' She dragged herself to her feet. 'I'm tired, Patrick, I think I'll go to bed.'

Patrick jumped up and seized her in his arms. 'Not so fast. Tell me one more thing, little wife. After seeing Bradley Stephenson the Third again tonight, do you still hanker after your Ivy League lover?'

Carey laid her head against his chest like a weary child. 'He was never my lover, Patrick.'

'That doesn't answer my question.' He put a finger under her chin and raised her face to his. 'Do you still feel the same about him?'

She gazed up into his fierce black eyes thoughtfully. 'Why are you so upset, Patrick? You always knew there was someone else. When you suggested marriage, remember, it was only because you wanted security for Alice.'

He looked at her in silence, his jaw clenched. 'I know that was the original plan,' he said at last. 'But it didn't turn out quite like that, did it?'

'No.'

'You know I'm fond of you.'

'Yes.'

'Are you fond of me?'

'Yes.'

His arms tightened. 'And *my* kisses?' he demanded hoarsely. 'Are they so abhorrent compared with your All-American Romeo?'

She shook her head dumbly, hypnotised by his glittering black stare.

'I'm *upset*,' he said between his teeth, 'because I'm so jealous I can't see straight. And one is only jealous, it is generally believed, when the physical attraction between two people is as powerful as it is between you and me, my angel. Or do you deny how good it is between us?'

Carey shook her head again, slowly, her eyelids growing heavy with the heat which was beginning to spread through her as Patrick held her closer and closer, one long hand beginning to caress her spine. His fingers slid downwards over the gold brocade, moving lower and lower until suddenly he cupped her bottom and pulled her hard against him. She gasped and he laughed softly, bending his head so that his lips remained a breath away from hers.

'Did *he* make you tremble like this, Carey? Did you make little choked noises in your throat for him, too?'

'Don't!' She trembled wildly as Patrick's mouth moved in hot demand down her throat. He thrust his hands in her hair, pulling out the remaining pins and tossing them aside. As the long black strands tumbled over her shoulders Patrick turned her in his arms, tugging down the long zip of the dress until the gold fabric fell to the floor and he lifted her clear of it, his eyes igniting in a face suddenly colourless, as the dying fire backlit creamy skin and filmy black lace and glossy, cascading hair.

With a stifled sound he pulled her to him, kissing her as though he meant to erase any last lingering memory she had of another man's kisses, to put his own personal stamp on her for all time, and Carey, all her emotions heightened to a painful degree by the events of the past few hours, responded to him utterly, with a new, wildfire response which blotted out everything and everyone in the world. As their hearts hammered together Patrick reached out behind him and locked the door, never taking his mouth from hers. He moved with her to the sofa and sank down with her among the cushions, and moments later the black lace lay discarded with formal black broadcloth on the floor as they came together in a fierce union which burned even as it healed the hurts inflicted by the painful revelations of the night.

When the storm was over Patrick picked his wife up in his arms and carried her upstairs to bed, where Carey, still in need of physical contact, thrust herself into her husband's arms with a fervour Patrick found as ravishing as it was novel. Unfailingly responsive though she'd been since their honeymoon, Patrick had nevertheless resigned himself to the constant role of instigator in their lovemaking up to now. Tonight, after the shock encounter with Brad, Carey's reaction was as unexpected as it was reassuring.

As the slender, naked body burrowed against him, Patrick's arms closed round her. He laughed breathlessly. 'After the hour we've just spent downstairs, plus giving you a lift up here, I ought to be done for, Madam Wife!'

'Are you?' whispered Carey, putting her lips against his throat.

Patrick was quiet for a moment. 'No,' he said in a stifled voice. 'I don't fancy I am.'

Carey wriggled higher, and kissed him on the mouth. 'Aren't you sure?'

'I am now!' He thrust her away from him for a moment. 'Carey—is all this some kind of apology?'

She bounced upright in bed, switching on the bedside lamp so he could see her face. She pushed her tumbled hair back and stared straight down into Patrick's quizzical eyes. 'Let's get one thing straight, right now. I did fall for Brad. Flat on my face, I suppose. I'd never felt like that for anyone before, so I was utterly convinced I could never want a sexual relationship with another man. But then I married you, and I was wrong. Now where I come from, Mr Savage, marriage means keeping to certain rules, so I promise never to hanker after Brad again. But at the same time I can't just throw a switch and black out *everything* I once felt for him. You've taught me that it's perfectly possible to feel attracted physically to more than one man— but I already knew it must be only one man at a time. Speech over.'

Patrick reached up and switched off the light before pulling her down into his arms. 'Right. Subject closed. Now, can we go back to about five minutes ago. You had your arms here, and I had mine here—is that right?'

'Approximately.'

He kissed her lingeringly, smoothing back her hair with one hand. 'Let's get something else straight, too, my angel,' he said against her lips. 'If by any chance the guy takes it into his head to renew his acquaintance with my wife I'll knock his teeth down his throat.'

'It wouldn't enter his head,' said Carey crossly, and pulled away. 'So kiss me goodnight and let's go to sleep.'

'I thought we were making love.'

'So did I. But you keep on talking.'

'Not another word!'

Patrick abandoned conversation and began to kiss and caress her with all the skill at his command. Carey closed her eyes, consigning a certain dark, accusing face from her mind and her life forever as she gave herself up to the bliss of Patrick's expert lovemaking, which was less frenzied and desperate than the first time. Now he had leisure to exert complete mastery over her, ignoring her smothered pleas as he made love to her with a slow, mounting intensity which had her crying for mercy as he brought her to the very brink of ecstasy time and time again before plunging with her over the edge into a turbulent sea of rapture, holding her fast in his arms as the tide receded and sleep overcame them at last.

CHAPTER NINE

CAREY woke next morning to someone pulling on her hair. She turned her head drowsily to smile into a pair of bright black eyes. 'Hello, honeybun. Where's Daddy?'

The small girl wriggled down in the bed, staking her claim. 'All gone,' she announced.

'No, I haven't,' contradicted Patrick, coming in to deposit a cup of tea beside Carey. He was fully dressed in heavy sweater and cord trousers, and had obviously showered and shaved and was ready for the day. He smiled down at his dishevelled wife. 'Good morning. Sorry about your visitor. I tried hard to be quiet but I woke madam here, I'm afraid.'

Carey smiled back sleepily. 'Why are you up so early?'

'I went to tidy the drawing-room.' His eyes danced. 'I had an idea Catriona might be shocked to find our clothes all over the floor.'

Carey flushed hotly. 'Heavens! I forgot all about them.'

He sat down on the bed and played idly with a lock of her hair. 'You were sleeping like the dead, so having disturbed this little charmer I dumped her in with you, then I got myself ready for the off.'

'Off?' Carey's eyes widened in dismay. 'Where are you going?'

'To Oxford for the day, sleepyhead! My presence is required—lord knows why—at the day's filming on location for my esteemed mini-series. Don't you remember? One of the Sunday glossies is sending a team to cover it for the paper, and P. Savage, Author, is part of the deal.'

'Oh, yes, of course. I just didn't think it was today.' Carey was utterly thrown by her deep dismay at the prospect. 'Will you be very late?' she asked, her eyes falling.

'Will you miss me if I am?'

'Desperately.'

Patrick's eyes darkened. 'Then I'll be early,' he promised huskily, and bent to kiss her. Forgetting about her little bedfellow, Carey reached up to put her arms round his neck and kissed him back with such unusual lack of inhibition that Patrick's arms locked about her convulsively.

Then Alice began to clamour for a hug too, and the farewell deteriorated into a romp, as Patrick enveloped his wife and daughter in a communal hug, from which he was obliged to extricate himself with reluctance before making for the door. He smiled at Carey ruefully.

'Just as well we've got company—otherwise I'd never tear myself away.'

Carey gathered the little girl close, smiling at Patrick over Alice's silver-gilt curls. 'Drive carefully.'

'Carey——' he began, then stopped, shaking his head. 'No. No time now. We'll talk tonight.'

'Something wrong?'

'No. Something very right, I hope.' Patrick glanced over his shoulder through the open doorway. 'I hear sounds of stirring below, so get some clothes on, Mrs Savage.'

'The moment you've gone,' she promised demurely.

'Spoilsport!' He gave her a gleaming grin, then ran downstairs, shouting a greeting to Catriona before the front door slammed behind him.

The day was cold and bright, and later, to give Carey some peace to wrap presents, Catriona took Alice out in her pushchair, making for the nearby gardens for a gossip with various others of her ilk who met there with their charges most fine mornings. Alone in the house, Carey had time to assess her own feelings at last, her mind busy as she wrestled with wrapping-paper and wrote on labels. It gave her a very odd feeling to realise she'd not only experienced the unthinkable by way of running into Bradley Stephenson again, but had survived it to tell the tale, quite literally, to Patrick. But the oddest thing of all, she thought with guilt, was to find herself so strangely unaffected by the encounter as far as Brad was concerned. Her marriage, it seemed, had certainly been the cure for the feeling she'd once felt would haunt her forever. At the time she had been convinced it was love. Now, if she was brutally honest with herself, her forbidden love seemed more like a schoolgirl crush. Mortifying.

Carey stowed her pile of parcels away in a safe place and went to look at herself in the gilt Venetian mirror over the mantel in the drawing-room. It was certainly no broken-hearted creature who looked back at her with quizzical grey eyes. The woman in the mirror, of course, was not the Miss Carey Armitage once known to Brad Stephenson. The girl in the reflection was quite definitely Mrs Patrick Savage, with a glowing confidence acquired only since her marriage.

Even her clothes were different. Carey eyed her scarlet cashmere sweater and black velvet trousers with a pleasure heightened by the fact that both items had been chosen by Patrick, as had the tasselled, flat suede shoes, even the way her hair was caught back by a scarlet velvet ribbon instead of twisted up into the prim knot Patrick objected to so fiercely.

The crux of the matter, Carey decided, eyes narrowed, was the desperate loss of self-respect she'd felt at finding herself physically attracted to a man who had not only been married, but had also happened to be her employer and the father of the children she'd looked after. It had taken her a long, long time to recover from the trauma of lowering the standards of her upbringing. It had been no help at all to remind herself that Brad Stephenson had been the first man to arouse a physical longing in her—a longing so fierce at the time she'd been utterly sure no man could ever take his place.

Which, of course, was why the marriage to Patrick had seemed so appealing afterwards. The idea of security and undemanding companionship and the satisfaction of being deeply needed as a mother to Alice had been balm to her soul. She frowned at herself blackly in the mirror. Was she shallow and promiscuous, then, to have succumbed to her husband's attraction so quickly? Or was Brad the fantasy and Patrick the reality? It had certainly seemed that way last night. Her reaction to Brad had been mostly dismay and guilt, nothing more, she realised, biting her lip. The sight of him had knocked her for six, true enough, not because she'd been flooded anew with guilty longing for him, but because she'd been so horribly afraid of how Patrick would react to it. Her relief on discovering that her husband had been blazing with jealousy rather than angry distaste had been so profound she'd responded to his lovemaking at first out of passionate gratitude.

Carey's eyes dilated as she glanced towards the sofa, her mouth drying as she remembered how the full force of her husband's expert tutelage had speedily metamorphosed gratitude into a passionate frenzy which surpassed anything she'd ever imagined she could feel. Her lips parted in a dreamy smile as she wondered how long she'd been deluding herself about her feelings for Patrick. If it had taken the sight of Brad Stephenson to show her how much she cared for her new husband, she had reason to be grateful to her former employer, rather than regarding him as the man who'd blighted her life.

The return of Alice and Catriona put an end to her musings, but later on in the morning Carey felt no great surprise when Ellen Stephenson rang, urging her to bring Patrick to dine with them at their hotel the first evening they were free.

Shuddering at the mere thought, Carey played for time by pretending to consult with a diary. 'I'm afraid that won't be until the first week in January, Ellen,' she fibbed. 'Patrick's in such demand at the moment.'

'Oh, honey!' wailed Ellen. 'We'll be in Germany by then.'

'What a shame.' Carey sent up a silent prayer as she suggested the Stephensons, children included, come round for tea one afternoon instead.

Her prayer was answered. Brad it seemed, just as Carey had counted on, was tied up during the day until Christmas.

'Couldn't you bring them without him?' suggested Carey, euphoric with relief. 'I'll be in this afternoon if you're free. I'd just love to see Dean and Abby again—and meet little Brad, of course.'

This was seized on with enthusiasm by Ellen Stephenson, who arrived swathed in furs later in the afternoon, with boisterous, blond Dean and dark, serious Abby, plus a solemn baby boy with Brad's blue eyes. Catriona was called in to help cope with the influx as Dean and Abby launched themself on Carey, hugging her and demanding her undivided attention for a while, which Alice objected to with vociferous jealousy. But after a time the children got on fairly well together once Alice had firmly established who was queen of the territory. Small though she was, the assertive personality inherited from her father soon had the American children enslaved, and Ellen and Carey were left in peace to drink tea and eat hot buttered muffins while they caught up with each other's news.

Ellen shook back her long blonde hair after a while, eyeing the diminutive, golden-haired Alice, who was bossing the others like a site foreman as they helped her build a castle from coloured blocks. 'I know I shouldn't say this, Carey honey,' she began. 'But how come you've got a baby this age? There doesn't seem to have been time——' She caught Carey's eye and blushed vividly. 'None of my business, of course——'

'Quite simple—I'm Alice's stepmother,' said Carey serenely. 'But I was her nanny before that.'

Ellen Stephenson's blue eyes looked puzzled. 'Did you know Patrick before he got divorced, then?'

'The first Mrs Savage died when the child was born, Ellen. I've been mother to Alice from the first.'

'Then she's a lucky little lady, Carey!' Ellen beamed. 'I'll tell Brad. He was real curious after Patrick mentioned a baby.'

I'll bet he was, thought Carey, and changed the subject adroitly to the proposed move to Hanover, and whether Ellen intended revisiting her favourite London shops, after which the afternoon passed quickly.

When it was time for the visitors to leave, Alice eyed Dean and Abby with hostility as they hugged Carey. She held up dimpled arms imperiously, clinging to Carey like a limpet as the visitors made their farewells, refusing to detach a hand even to wave bye-bye, as she normally did at the drop of a hat. As the taxi moved away Catriona closed the door and tried to relieve Carey of the child, but Alice was having none of it.

'Mum-mum,' she said stormily, and clung tighter.

Carey smiled down into the flushed little face. 'It's all right, Catriona. We'll cuddle up on the sofa and read about Miffy the Rabbit for a while. Alice is a bit jealous, I think.'

Just like her father, thought Carey with a secret little smile as the Scots girl went off to enjoy half an hour to herself before Alice's bathtime. Not long afterwards Patrick rang to say he'd been delayed and not to wait for dinner, as he'd be late. Carey was disappointed and, unusually, let him know she was.

'Not half as much as I am, Carey.' The familiar drawl became very pronounced. 'But I'll be home by bedtime, I promise.'

Carey went into the kitchen to inform Catriona of the change of plan. 'Let's leave the roast until tomorrow night and have bacon and eggs or something quick and sinful instead, shall we? After those muffins I'm not very hungry anyway.'

Catriona smiled. 'Fine by me, Mrs Savage. Is it all right if I go out later, when Alice is in bed?'

'Of course.' Carey became aware that the child was growing heavy in her arms. 'Hey, honeybun, bathtime now.'

Later, when Alice was settled, Carey had a swift bath before Catriona was to take off for the cinema with a French au pair who worked for a neighbouring family. She heard the telephone a couple of times while she was in the bathroom, and went downstairs in her dressing-gown afterwards to ask if Patrick had been one of the callers.

'No, Mrs Savage.' Catriona looked up with a smile from her ironing. 'One was Antoinette checking if it was all right for tonight, and the other was some man selling double glazing.'

Carey laughed and hurried back upstairs, taking her time over choosing something to wear. Tonight she was determined to look her best when Patrick came home, and, since he'd bought her a lot of new clothes lately, the choice took much longer than it would have done before her marriage. Patrick was a very tactile man, always wanting to smooth her hair or touch her hand, unable to resist patting her bottom whenever it was in range, and he loved textures, velvet most of all. Since there was a good fire in the drawing-room Carey decided to be lazy and put on the new green velvet dressing-gown which looked almost like an evening dress with its wide satin sash. Her only other garments were an ivory satin teddy and a pair of flat green velvet slippers, and she smiled mischievously as she pictured Patrick's reaction when he came home. Despite her dishabille she took a long time over her face and hair, securing the latter behind her ears with combs and letting it hang down her back. She eyed the result, then on impulse put outsized gold hoops in her ears and slid on the heavy gold bangle Patrick had bought her in Lisbon on the way home from their honeymoon. That should do it, she decided, kissing her hand to herself in the mirror before going into the nursery to look at Alice, who was fast asleep in an abandoned little heap after the excitement of the afternoon.

Once Catriona had gone off to her film Carey was at a loss as to what to do with herself. She found it hard to settle to anything. Television, books, magazines—nothing kept her attention for long, and in the end she decided to hang a few ornaments on the Christmas tree delivered late that afternoon. It stood tall in the hallway, taking up far too much space in Carey's opinion, but to have it anywhere else was out of the question at Alice's present stage of relentless investigation of her surroundings. Her costume not designed for mountaineering, Carey began on the branches she could reach without recourse to a chair, smiling as she hung glass baubles and chocolate Santas well out of Alice's reach. Carey put some music on Patrick's stereo, humming along with Bill Withers' 'Lovely Day' as she warmed to her task. She was halfway up the tree when the doorbell rang. Her eyes lit up. Patrick was early and had forgotten his key, a regular habit of his.

Carey threw open the door, then froze at the sight of Brad Stephenson on the shallow steps leading down into the street. For a moment they stared at each other in tense silence. Brad's craggy, handsome face looked all hollows and bones by the light of the lamp at the kerb, the appeal on it naked as he put out a hand towards her.

'Hello, Carey.'

She eyed him without pleasure. 'What on earth are you doing here, Brad?'

'Let me in, Carey—*please*? I just had to see you.'

Brad Stephenson looked tired and strained, with a lack of assurance about him Carey viewed with faint surprise as she stood aside unwillingly to let him pass into the hall.

'I'm afraid it can't be for long,' she told him, and closed the outer door, standing against it with arms folded defensively.

In the close confines of the hall Brad looked very large in his fur-lined greatcoat. He'd been a notable football quarterback in his college days, but looked heavier now than she remembered, Carey thought dispassionately. Probably because she was used to Patrick's thoroughbred leanness.

'Expecting company?' asked Brad, his eyes devouring her in a way which made her feel hideously uncomfortable.

'Yes.' Which was no more than the truth, after all. She was expecting Patrick later.

'You look great, Carey,' he said with a sigh, and moved towards her.

Carey brushed past him and led the way into the drawing-room. 'May I offer you a drink?'

He followed her quickly. 'I don't want a drink, Carey.'

'What *do* you want, Brad?' She turned to face him. 'If it was news of me you could have got that back at the hotel. Ellen was here with the children this afternoon.'

He grimaced. 'She had some fool idea of asking you and—and your celebrity husband to dinner.'

'So I gather—but we're not free before you leave town, I'm afraid.'

'Thank the lord for that,' he said bitterly. 'I came here to ask you to refuse. It breaks me up to see you and this Savage guy together.'

'I really don't see why it should,' said Carey, rather in the manner she'd once used to Dean and Abby.

'What I had to know was how the hell you had a baby so quickly,' he asked suddenly, his deep-set blue eyes accusing. 'You wouldn't sleep with me, then got yourself pregnant straight after by this other guy!'

'Ellen could have explained,' said Carey, deeply affronted. 'Alice is my stepdaughter. Patrick was a widower when I married him.'

There was a tense pause, while Brad stared at Carey as though he meant to imprint her features on his memory. 'Do you love him, Carey?' he said at last, as if it gave him physical pain to ask.

'Do you love Ellen?'

'That's different!'

'Is it?' Her chin lifted proudly. 'Actually I think you're right. Because I love Patrick in rather a different way from what you feel for your wife. Oddly enough, I didn't realise how much I do love him until I saw you again last night, because until then you'd been a big black shadow hanging over my life. I was so green and inexperienced when I met you. I actually thought, you see, that after you I'd never be capable of that kind of physical yearning for any other man ever again in my entire life.'

Hope leapt in his eyes for a moment, then died as he realised she wasn't finished.

'I was quite right,' said Carey, almost wonderingly as she realised the truth of it. 'I *don't* feel the same for Patrick as I did towards you.'

He lunged towards her, gripping her by the elbows. 'I knew it!' he said, his voice hoarse with triumph.

'Not so fast.' Carey disengaged herself very deliberately, noting with detachment that his touch meant nothing now. Strange, she thought sadly, and looked up into the face that had once haunted her dreams. 'I realise now that what I felt for you was some sort of puppy-love on my part, no more than a schoolgirl crush. Probably because you were the first man to wake me up to the fact that I even possessed a libido, Brad. But those guilty, immature longings I felt for you turned out to be just a sort of rehearsal for the way I feel for the man I married.'

'OK, OK,' he snapped, and rubbed a hand over his face. 'Put your knife away, Carey. You've made your point. But believe me, honey, I've felt very badly about you ever since the day you left us. Seeing you last night, looking so fantastic in that gold dress, with that guy hanging on to you like he was afraid someone would steal you away from him——' His fists clenched at his sides. 'It knocked me flat.'

Carey glanced at the clock nervously. 'Yes, well, now we've cleared all that up I think you should leave. You took a chance on finding me alone, anyway, Brad. Patrick's usually home at this hour.'

'Your maid said he wouldn't be here until later.' Brad gave her a twisted grin. 'I rang earlier, making out I peddled windows.'

Carey made a mental note to instruct Catriona to be less forthcoming about Patrick's whereabouts in future. She held out her hand formally. 'Goodbye, Brad. It was kind of you to call.'

'Kind! Hell—I just wanted...' He stopped, biting his lip.

Carey eyed him challengingly. 'What did you want, I wonder? Did you come here expecting to indulge in a little extra-marital fun and games again?'

Brad Stephenson flushed a dull red. 'That's not fair!'

'Life's not either, Brad.' Carey stiffened as a key sounded in the lock. 'Oh, dear lord. It's Patrick!' she said wildly.

Bradley Stephenson was no coward. He drew himself up, looking more composed than Carey, as Patrick Savage came into the room like a whirlwind, his arms outstretched to his wife.

'Sorry I'm late, darling...' He stopped dead as he saw that Carey had company. His hands fell to his sides as he eyed the American with cold animosity. 'Sorry. Didn't know we were expecting guests tonight.'

Carey went to him, standing on tiptoe to kiss him on the mouth. 'Hello, darling,' she said quickly, panicking at the look in his eyes. 'You remember Brad Stephenson, of course. We met last night at Sadie's.'

'Good evening,' said Patrick, with such deep-frozen formality that Brad's mouth twisted.

'Hi. Seems I got my wires crossed,' he said, the flat Boston vowels very pronounced. 'Came to collect my wife and children, but they'd already left.'

'Ellen brought Dean and Abby and little Brad round for tea,' said Carey jerkily, and linked her arm through Patrick's, which tensed like an iron bar beneath her hand.

'How nice for you,' said Patrick, never taking his eyes from the visitor's uneasy face. 'Drink, Stephenson?'

'No, thanks—my driver's waiting. I'd better get back to the hotel.' Brad turned to Carey. 'Great to see you again, Carey. Sorry you can't make it for dinner before we leave.' He held out his hand.

Carey took it, smiling politely. 'Goodbye, Brad. Good luck in Hanover.'

'Thanks.' He nodded at Patrick. 'Goodbye, Savage.'

'I'll see you to the door.' Without a look in Carey's direction Patrick, who was still in his heavy zippered suede jacket, ushered the other man out. Almost at once Carey heard the bang of the outer door and braced herself, waiting for Patrick to come back into the room. But to her dismay Patrick's footsteps, sounding slow and heavy, went past the door and along the hall and up the stairs, leaving her tense and desolate all by herself. For several fraught minutes she waited in front of the fire, sure he'd come back. But after a while it became clear he had no intention of coming back.

Now what? Should she run after him? Explain? If she did would he even listen, let alone believe her? Nevertheless she had to try. Carey marched to the door with purpose, then heard a familiar cry as she reached the hall. She flew upstairs and along the landing to Alice's room, where the little girl was standing up in her cot, holding on to the bars.

'Drink,' she said imperiously.

'Sit down then, honeybun,' instructed Carey as she poured juice from a thermos into a beaker. 'Now. What else do you say?'

The child thought for a moment, then as the beaker remained out of her reach she smiled cajolingly, looking so like Patrick that Carey's heart lurched. *'Please!'* said Alice in triumph, plopping down on her bottom.

'What a good girl,' said Carey huskily, leaning on the cot rail as she watched her stepdaughter drinking thirstily, forehead furrowed with concentration as Alice gripped the beaker with two fat little cupped hands.

'All gone!' announced Alice, handing the beaker back, and Carey laughed a little unsteadily.

'Thank you, darling. Now go to sleep.' She bent to tuck the child in, but Alice bounced up again suddenly, her face wreathed in smiles.

'Daddy!'

Carey turned quickly to see Patrick in his dressing-gown behind her, his hair slick and wet from a shower.

'Hello, poppet.' He lifted his daughter out of the cot and held her tight, his eyes boring into Carey's over the bright gold head. 'Have you been a good girl?' he asked very softly.

Alice nodded, burrowing against his towelling-clad shoulder sleepily, and Patrick kissed the top of her head then laid her down in the cot.

'Goodnight, poppet.'

Alice yawned, flapping a small hand at them both as she settled against her pillow. 'Bye-bye.'

Carey bent to kiss the flushed cheek, covered the child up, then turned away, her heart heavy at the shuttered look on Patrick's face as he followed her from the room.

'Have you had dinner?' she asked.

'All I want. I'll be down in a few minutes. Could you make some coffee? I'd like a word with you, Carey,' said Patrick, his face as informative as a blank page.

'Yes,' said Carey to both, and went down to the kitchen to do as he'd asked. When she arrived in the drawing-room, tray in hand, Patrick was there before her, punctiliously polite as he relieved her of her burden and set it down on the sofa table.

'I have something to say to you, too, Patrick,' she said, deciding to carry the war into the enemy's camp. She looked up to surprise a leap of despair in his eyes before his lids came down to hide it.

'I'm listening,' he said very quietly as he accepted a cup of coffee. He sat down opposite her, his long legs stretched out in front of him as he looked across at her in question. 'I imagine it's something to do with Stephenson.'

'No. Absolutely nothing.' Carey returned the look squarely, almost amused by the blankness on Patrick's face. 'But perhaps you'd rather have your word first.'

'My word?'

'The one you mentioned upstairs.'

Patrick looked morose. 'All right. Why was Stephenson here? He can't have expected me to believe that cock-and-bull story about collecting his wife and children from a tea-party at eight o'clock at night.'

'No. Probably it was the first thing that came into his head. Although,' added Carey, 'Ellen did bring the children here this afternoon. But naturally they'd gone long since. Brad didn't even know they were coming.'

'So he nipped in here for a little chat on his way home to the bosom of his family,' he said, his voice heavy with sarcasm.

'Yes.'

'What the hell do you mean by "yes"?'

Carey leaned back in the deep, comfortable chair, feeling suddenly weary. 'I suppose I mean that whatever his motive for coming here, a chat was all he got, Patrick, whether you believe me or not.'

'I do believe you,' he said, surprising her.

Carey lifted her head and gazed across at him, her eyes holding his. 'Why, Patrick?'

The sudden intimacy of his smile made her heart skip a beat. 'You forget, Carey, that I, better than anyone, know exactly how you look when a man's just been making love to you.'

'Oh!'

'And perhaps I'm deluding myself, of course, but apart from the embarrassment on your face I could have sworn you were glad to see me. Which is more than could have been said for your visitor,' he added acidly. 'I got the distinct impression that Mr Stephenson hates my guts, Carey. Dog-in-the-manger type, would you say?'

Carey shrugged. 'I wouldn't know—though I do know why he wanted to talk to me. Both Ellen and Brad on their separate visits, and for very different reasons, were wildly curious to know how I managed to produce a child so quickly—the child *you* implied was ours.'

'Petty on my part, but damned satisfying!' Patrick grinned wolfishly. 'The idea was not, I fancy, one which appealed to your jealous philanderer one bit. Nor was he exceptionally pleased when I put in an appearance tonight, either.'

'I'm not surprised,' retorted Carey. 'You weren't exactly friendly.'

'Hell and damnation!' exploded Patrick, jumping up. 'What did you expect, woman?' He stopped dead in the middle of the room, and swung round on her suddenly. '*Did* he touch you, Carey?'

'No.'

Patrick slumped down in his chair again, looking morose. 'Did you want him to?'

'No.'

There was silence for a moment, then Patrick sighed heavily. 'All right, Carey, what was it you wanted to say to me?'

Carey hesitated, her eyes holding his. 'I thought you'd like to know I'm pregnant,' she said at last, then shrank back in her chair at the extraordinary effect her statement had on Patrick. He shot from his own chair like a catapult and leapt across the room to hang above her, one hand on each of the arms of her chair as his eyes bored down into hers.

'You're what?' he shouted, his voice cracking.

'Patrick! You'll wake Alice,' said Carey in utter dismay.

'I don't believe it!' He shuddered, and turned away to lean against the mantelshelf, his face in the crook of his arm. 'I never even thought to ask—I assumed——'

Carey felt her temper rise. 'Oh, I see! It was *my* responsibility to make sure it wouldn't happen! Well, I didn't. We were supposed to have a platonic marriage, remember. Birth control didn't come up on the agenda.'

Patrick turned to her with a look of such anguish on his face that her heart contracted. 'Carey, you don't have to go through with this.'

She glared at him, her grey eyes glittering like ice. 'I do, you know.'

'There are ways——'

'None I consider even remotely possible.' Carey lifted her chin, feeling as though her heart had died inside her. 'It's not something I did out of malice, you know—nor did I manage it on my own, Patrick Savage. I'm sorry you feel like this——'

'You don't know the least damn thing about how I feel!' Patrick sank down on his knees beside her chair, grabbing at her hands. 'Carey, I've been through it once—for pity's sake don't put me through it again.' He lifted her hands to his lips, then looked up at her with eyes which burned. 'Surely you must know by now how much I love you? That no baby is worth even the thought that I might lose you?'

A great frozen lump inside Carey melted. 'Oh, is *that* all,' she said, giddy with relief as she smiled at him.

Patrick pulled her out of her chair, shaking her slightly. 'Be serious, woman! Listen to me—I didn't know what love was until I met you, Carey. And maybe it sounds too bloody melodramatic for words, but if you died too, like Stephanie, as a direct result of—of our relationship, I think I'd cut my throat.'

'You're right—that *is* melodramatic—*and* preposterous. Look—for Stephanie it was very different.' Carey reached up to cup his face, her eyes blazing so fiercely that Patrick's closed, dazzled by them. 'But this is me, Carey, and not only am I as healthy as a horse, but about sixteen years younger than Stephanie, and I am also quite determined to have your baby for a great number of reasons, not least of which is the fact that I love you with all my heart and soul—and the rest of me, too,' she added with a crooked grin, and kissed him.

Patrick groaned and held her cruelly close, returning the kiss with a hunger fed by several warring emotions. 'Have you any idea,' he demanded, when he tore his mouth away, 'how it makes me feel to have you admit you love me?'

'I think so—if it's anything like the way I feel to know you love *me*!'

He examined her flushed, jubilant face with such possessive eyes her colour deepened even further. 'I was afraid the "word" you had to say to me was goodbye, you know.'

Carey looked astonished. 'But why?'

'I was deadly afraid Mr Bradley Stephenson the bloody Third had come here tonight to throw up his family and career and gallop off with you into the sunset.'

She roared with laughter. 'If you put that sort of thing in your books, Mr Savage, you'd never get in the top ten!' She took his hand and pushed him down on the sofa, then curled up alongside him in the crook of his arm. 'Such a thing would never have entered Brad's head, I assure you.'

'Then why the hell *did* he come here tonight?' demanded Patrick angrily. 'For one thing how did he know you'd be alone?' He twisted round, almost rough with her as he raised her face to his. 'Did you tell him?'

Carey shoved at him in fury. 'No, I did not! If you must know he rang up while I was in the bath, pretending he was selling double glazing. Catriona told him you wouldn't be home until later.'

'Did he now!' Patrick's eyes blazed. 'I'd better have a word with your Mr Stephenson——'

'No, Patrick, please,' Carey implored.

'Why? Are you worried I might hurt him?' he demanded, incensed.

'No. I'm worried you—or I—might hurt Ellen. I went to great lengths to avoid that the last time, so what point is there in risking it now?' Carey smiled up into his tense face. 'I'm fond of Ellen.'

'And Brad? How do you feel about him?'

Carey met his eyes very squarely. 'I feel a bit worried about that.'

Patrick went white. 'What—what do you mean?'

'Well, I made such a song and dance about him to myself for a while, utterly convinced no other man would ever mean the same to me as him.' Carey hesitated, her eyes troubled. 'Then when I saw him last night so unexpectedly——'

'I thought you were going to faint!'

She threw her arms round his neck. 'But that was because I was afraid of how *you'd* react, Patrick. One look at him and all I could think of was that my life could be ruined a second time. Only this time I'd never recover because I'd lose *you*. And that, my darling husband, would be a tragedy I'd never get over. Ever.'

Patrick let out a long, unsteady breath and kissed her until both their hearts were hammering. 'You won't lose me, I promise,' he warned at last, looking suddenly grim. 'Particularly under the present circumstances. I'm not going to let you out of my sight until the baby's born.'

'Patrick!' Carey pushed him away irritably. 'Nothing will go wrong, I promise. And it'll be a jolly good thing for Alice to have a new baby in the house. She's in imminent danger of becoming spoiled rotten—by both of us.'

'True.' Patrick drew her back against him. 'But don't let's think of Alice, or even the new baby for the moment. Let's just talk about us.'

Carey was in full agreement. She smiled up into Patrick's possessive face. 'You never did say why you got home early after all.'

'I was in a hurry to tell you I love you,' he said simply, the look in his eyes making her tremble. 'I almost did this morning, but Alice rather got in the

way, if you remember. Mind you, I've been on the
point of telling you for ages—lord knows how I've
kept it back. Particularly last night.' He kissed her
hard. 'To have you respond to me so fiercely,
sweetheart, was an experience even more wonderful than anything that had gone before.'

Carey smiled radiantly. 'I'm glad, because I felt
the same. For me it was as though a great shackle
had fallen off and I was free to love you as you
should be loved—with everything I have to give.'

'Because you realised you were no longer in love
with Stephenson?'

Carey's eyes glittered suddenly. 'Oh, no. I was
deprived of any illusions on that score the day I
left my job. My *mind* had been free of Brad for a
long time. What I found so hard to bear, not to
mention degrading, was the fact that I hankered
after his kisses—sometimes indulged in little day-
dreams about what it would have been like to have
him as a lover. Heavens, how naïve that sounds!'

Patrick held her close. 'I keep on wondering
about that final straw which had you running from
the Stephensons. Tell me about it.'

She sighed. 'It seems so stupid now. I can hardly
credit how stupid. You may remember that when
Brad kissed me he told me he'd been crazy about
me for months, and I believed him implicitly, so
flattered I couldn't see straight. But next day I came
down to earth with a bump. Ellen was shattered
because I was leaving, pleaded with me to go back
to her as soon as I could because she was eight
weeks pregnant!' Carey gave a shaky little laugh.
'What a fool I was. It cut me to the heart to think

that Brad had been making love to his wife the whole time he made out he'd been in love with me!'

Patrick cursed colourfully under his breath, then held her away from him. 'Are you *sure* you don't want me to punch the bastard in the nose?'

'Quite sure—thanks just the same,' said Carey, kissing him in passionate gratitude for the offer.

Patrick was quiet for a time as he held her close.

'What are you thinking?' asked Carey uneasily, worried he was disgusted by her confessions.

'I was thinking that it's time you had a nanny for Alice,' he announced.

'Certainly not!' Carey drew away from him, glaring. 'I've always looked after Alice.'

'You haven't always been pregnant,' he reminded her, thrusting a hand through his hair.

Carey calmed down. 'Perhaps later on,' she amended.

'No. Now. Alice is more than bright enough to realise she's being handed over to a nanny because of the new baby, don't you think? In which case she'll probably murder it! Besides,' added Patrick with a sidelong glance, 'I think you should take it easy. Put your feet up more often.' He sighed heavily.

'What's the matter now?'

'I had different ideas about the climax of this evening, Mrs Savage. I was going to fall on one knee, declare my love and carry you off to bed and spend all night making love to you.'

'So?'

'Now I'd better rewrite the scenario—at least the last bit.'

Carey jumped to her feet, and stood glaring at her husband crossly. 'I've taken enormous care with my face and hair—not though you'd know it after your attentions. I am also wearing shamelessly little under this garment you bought me, yet after all that the only thing you can talk about is putting my feet up. I'm pregnant, not incapacitated.' She eyed him stormily. 'I was pregnant last night, too, remember!'

'So you were.' Patrick looked up at her, as if he were seeing the new green velvet for the first time. 'And now I come to think of it, would you kindly choose something less provocative to receive visitors in future? You look a damn sight too tempting in that, Carey.'

'I'm pleased to hear it. Though it wasn't visitors I set out to tempt. It was you!'

'In which case I suppose it does seem a bit on the discourteous side to feign an indifference I sure as hell don't feel.'

Carey nodded vigorously. 'I'd be deeply offended. Hell hath no fury, and all that.'

'I wasn't scorning you, darling—only trying, unsuccessfully, to keep a rein on my baser instincts!'

'You mean we're back to square one again, then,' she said, sighing.

'What do you mean?'

'I'm talking about that civilised arrangement of yours—the one that didn't last very long!'

Carey watched, surprised, as a rare look of indecision passed over Patrick's face.

Then he stood up and squared his shoulders, with the air of someone about to make a confession.

'Since this seems to be the night for revelations I suppose I'd better come clean. I put my proposal of marriage to you in those particular terms, Carey, purely because I was certain it was the only kind you'd consider.'

Her eyebrows shot into her hair. 'You mean you never had any intention of keeping to the platonic bit?'

His eyes glittered guiltily. 'Shall we say I hoped against hope I wouldn't be obliged to. Lord, Carey, I'm only human.'

'You told me your libido was sort of in abeyance,' she said accusingly.

'It had been! Frankly I was quite convinced at one stage that I'd never feel anything for a woman again during that nightmare period after Stephanie died. No matter how many gorgeous creatures the Morgans brought along to brighten my voluntary exile in California, I never felt the slightest flicker of interest in any of them. It depressed the hell out of me.'

'Shock does strange things,' said Carey, and slid her arms round his waist, leaning back to look up at him. 'So when did you first find out that this affliction of yours wasn't permanent after all?'

Patrick's expressive mouth twisted in a very strange smile. 'Oddly enough, I can pin-point it to the actual second.' His arms tightened round her. 'It was about two in the morning last June.'

Carey's eyes narrowed. 'Which morning?'

'You must remember, darling—you were there!' Patrick's eyes danced. 'I was sitting on the kitchen table in Llynglas, drinking coffee, when in burst a barefoot creature with her hair hanging down her back, big grey eyes like saucers at the sight of me. And—well, I don't know quite how to put this politely, but one look at you, Carey, and I was left in no doubt whatsoever that my worries were over!'

Bright colour flooded her laughing face, then she turned on him. 'Is that why you married me, then? Because I restored you to—er—life, as it were? *I* thought it was to provide a mother for Alice.'

Patrick sobered. 'Alice needed one, heaven knows, but that wasn't the main reason, however much I piled on the agony about it to persuade you. I asked you to marry me for the simple reason that I fell in love with you, darling. I knew you didn't love me, of course, also that you were carrying a highly inconvenient torch for someone else. Which is why I hit on the idea of a platonic arrangement. I thought it was the only one you were likely to agree to. I confess I used Alice as enticement, but then, I was ready to bribe you any way I could, Carey. And,' he added, with a steely glint in his eye, 'I had no doubt whatsoever that, given time, I'd be able to make you forget all about the mystery man you were languishing over.'

Carey felt such joy flooding through her at his confession she felt confident enough to tease a little. 'Tell me, if I hadn't decided to make our marriage more—more normal, Patrick, would you have gone on keeping to your promise about the sleeping arrangements?'

'I *hope* I would have,' he said carefully, then his eyes danced again. 'Let's say it was a jolly good thing my restraint wasn't tested any longer than it was!'

Carey slid her arms round his neck, bringing his bright head down to hers. 'Now then, husband dear, I think it's time we began to discuss a new kind of arrangement.'

Patrick stiffened against her, his eyes slitted suspiciously. 'What is it?'

Carey kissed her husband lovingly. 'All it entails is a normal, loving relationship between Mr P. Savage and Mrs C. Savage, with no shadows from the past to spoil it—and no silly qualms about Mrs Savage's present condition. Do I make myself clear?'

Patrick eyed her challenging face then smiled, elation in his gaze even as he admitted defeat. 'OK. I agree—but only because I like your arrangement a whole lot better than mine!'

Carey leaned against her husband, blissfully happy as they left the lower floor in darkness and climbed the stairs, arms about each other, their laughter stilled for a moment as they went in to peep at Alice, who lay, arms outflung, angelic as a gilt-haired cherub in her sleep.

'How lucky I am,' said Carey later with a sigh, as Patrick closed their bedroom door. He shook his head, his smile triumphantly possessive as he took her in his arms.

'Wrong, my darling wife. As I've said before— *I'm* the lucky one!'

Fall in love with

Harlequin Superromance®

Passionate.
Love that strikes like lightning. Drama that will touch your heart.

Provocative.
As new and exciting as today's headlines.

Poignant.
Stories of men and women like you. People who affirm the values of loving, caring and commitment in today's complex world.

At 300 pages, Superromance novels will give you even more hours of enjoyment.

Look for four new titles every month.

Harlequin Superromance
"Books that will make you laugh and cry."

PENNY JORDAN

Sins and infidelities . . .
Dreams and obsessions . . .
Shattering secrets
unfold in . . .

THE HIDDEN YEARS

SAGE — stunning, sensual and
vibrant, she spent a lifetime
distancing herself from a past too
painful to confront . . . the mother
who seemed to hold her at bay,
the father who resented her and
the heartache of unfulfilled love.
To the world, Sage was
independent and invulnerable—
but it was a mask she cultivated to
hide a desperation she herself
couldn't quite understand . . .
until an unforeseen turn of events
drew her into the discovery of the
hidden years, finally allowing
Sage to open her heart to a
passion denied for so long.

The Hidden Years—a compelling novel of truth and passion
that will unlock the heart and soul of every woman.

AVAILABLE IN OCTOBER!
Watch for your opportunity to complete your Penny Jordan set.
POWER PLAY and SILVER will also be available in October.

HIDDEN